ROSES

FOR

MAMA

Books by Janette Oke

*Another Homecoming**
*Tomorrow's Dream**

CANADIAN WEST
When Calls the Heart *When Breaks the Dawn*
When Comes the Spring *When Hope Springs New*
Beyond the Gathering Storm
When Tomorrow Comes

LOVE COMES SOFTLY
Love Comes Softly *Love's Unending Legacy*
Love's Enduring Promise *Love's Unfolding Dream*
Love's Long Journey *Love Takes Wing*
Love's Abiding Joy *Love Finds a Home*

A PRAIRIE LEGACY
The Tender Years *A Quiet Strength*
A Searching Heart *Like Gold Refined*

SEASONS OF THE HEART
Once Upon a Summer *Winter Is Not Forever*
The Winds of Autumn *Spring's Gentle Promise*

SONG OF ACADIA*
The Meeting Place *The Birthright*
The Sacred Shore *The Distant Beacon*
The Beloved Land

WOMEN OF THE WEST
The Calling of Emily Evans *A Bride for Donnigan*
Julia's Last Hope *Heart of the Wilderness*
Roses for Mama *Too Long a Stranger*
A Woman Named Damaris *The Bluebird and the Sparrow*
They Called Her Mrs. Doc *A Gown of Spanish Lace*
The Measure of a Heart *Drums of Change*

———

Janette Oke: A Heart for the Prairie
Biography of Janette Oke by Laurel Oke Logan

*with T. Davis Bunn

JANETTE OKE

ROSES
— FOR —
MAMA

BETHANYHOUSE

MINNEAPOLIS, MINNESOTA

Roses for Mama
Copyright © 1991
Janette Oke

Cover design by Lookout Design Group, Inc.

Published by Bethany House Publishers
11400 Hampshire Avenue South
Bloomington, Minnesota 55438

Bethany House Publishers is a division of
Baker Publishing Group, Grand Rapids, Michigan.

Printed in the United States of America

ISBN-13: 978-0-7642-0246-9
ISBN-10: 0-7642-0246-4

The Library of Congress has cataloged the original edition as follows:

Oke, Janette, 1935-
    Roses for Mama / Janette Oke.
        p.   cm.
    ISBN 1-55661-185-4 (pbk.) — ISBN 1-55661-199-4 (large print pbk.)
    I. Title
PR9199.3.038R67   1991
813'.54—dc20   91-8659
                                                                    CIP

To Mother,

Amy Marie Ruggles Steeves,

from one of your bouquet of eight.

JANETTE OKE was born in Champion, Alberta, to a Canadian prairie farmer and his wife, and she grew up in a large family full of laughter and love. She is a graduate of Mountain View Bible College in Alberta, where she met her husband, Edward, and they were married in May of 1957. After pastoring churches in Indiana and Canada, the Okes spent some years in Calgary, where Edward served in several positions on college faculties while Janette continued her writing. She has written over four dozen novels for adults and children, and her book sales total over twenty-two million copies.

The Okes have three sons and one daughter, all married, and are enjoying their dozen grandchildren. Edward and Janette are active in their local church and make their home near Didsbury, Alberta.

Contents

Chapter One

Angela

Angela Peterson wiped her hands on her dark blue apron, then reached up and tucked a wisp of blond hair into a side comb. It was a warm day, and the tub of hot water over which she had been leaning did not make it any cooler. She stretched to take some of the kink from her back and lifted her eyes to the back field where Thomas's breaking plow stitched a furrowed pattern. He would soon be in for his dinner.

Angela bent over the tub again and scrubbed the soiled socks with renewed vigor. She wanted to finish before stopping to put dinner on the table, and this was her last load.

"I hate washing socks," she fretted, then quickly bit her tongue as she recalled a soft voice: "Remember, never despise a task—any task. In doing any job, you are either creating something or bettering something."

Mama had always said things like that. Usually Angela grasped the truth of her words quickly, but sometimes her statements made Angela stiffen with a bit of rebellion. After giving the words some thought, though, she always came to understand their plain, common sense. As each year slipped by, Angela went back to the words of her mother more and more. Mama had not just spoken her thoughts to her children; she had lived the lessons before them. And Mama had been a living example of all the things that make a lady.

As usual, thoughts of Mama were followed quickly by thoughts of Papa, and Angela felt her eyes lifting up and up, as though Papa were suddenly standing before her. He was of Scandinavian stock. He was so tall—her papa. So tall and strong, with broad shoulders, sturdy forearms, and a straight, almost stiff back. His eyes were blue, like deep, icy water. "Like the fjords," Mama would say, then smile softly, and her children knew she considered the fjords something very special even though she had never seen them herself.

Angela smiled at the thought, then turned her attention back to the dirty sock on the washboard. The wind had strengthened and she had to stop again and brush silky strands of hair from her face. From across the valley came the sound of a ringing bell. The school children were being called in to resume their morning classes. And Angela resumed her scrubbing on the sock before her, wrung it out, and tossed it in the rinse tub. She swished a slender hand through the soapy water to locate the next one and sighed with relief when her hand came up empty.

Her back ached as she straightened, but she had no time to dwell on the discomfort. Another task called for her attention. Thomas would have heard the ringing school bell too—his signal to come in for dinner.

Hurriedly, Angela rinsed the footwear and pegged it to the line.

I'll leave the emptying until after we eat, she told herself as she hastened to the kitchen.

The house the Peterson family inhabited was not large, but neither was it crowded, even though five people lived there. On a bluff overlooking the valley, it was protected on three sides by poplar trees. From the front, the wide veranda looked out over open countryside way over to the slim spire of the town church, the only thing belonging to the town that they could see from their yard. Angela pictured the rest. The wide main street with narrower streets leading off to this side and that; the board sidewalks; the hardware store filled with hammers, shovels, and yard goods; the drugstore with its window display of hard candies; the grocery with barrels and bins of kitchen stock; the meat market with its sawdust-covered floor. Angela had never liked trips to the meat market. She didn't like the smell of meat until it was simmering in the big frying pan or sizzling in the roaster in the oven.

Angela had just enough time to put the left-over stew on to heat and set the table before she heard steps across the side porch. She turned to the loaf of bread she had placed on the cutting board and placed thick slices on a plate. Thomas was washing up at the blue basin and wiping dry on the wash-worn towel suspended from the roller.

Angela put the bread on the table and hurried back to the stove. The coffee still hadn't boiled and the stew was not yet bubbling.

"I'm sorry," she murmured softly over her shoulder, "I'm a bit slow. The washing seemed to take me longer today."

"I saw," Thomas responded. "The line's full. You need more clothesline?"

Angela shook her head and looked at Thomas, who had taken his place at the table. His face was shining with a just-washed look, but his hair was still tousled from the morning breezes.

"I don't think so—it just seemed that most everything was dirty this week. Don't know when Louise had so many dresses in the wash, and Derek had extra overalls, what with his mis-hap with the puddle and all. Then there was extra bedding with Sara having Bertha sleep over—and, well, it all just added up I guess."

Thomas nodded and leaned a muscled arm on the table.

Angela stirred the stew again and looked at Thomas. "You want it now—or hot."

"Hot," he answered without hesitation. "The horses need time to feed anyway. And I don't mind sitting a spell myself."

Angela left her spot by the stove and went to take the chair opposite Thomas.

"How's it going?" she asked simply.

"Looks good. Lots of spring moisture. Low places a bit wet yet."

"You going to try some of your new seed?"

Angela had never understood Thomas's love for experi-menting with the crops, but she allowed him his pleasure. And she was interested in anything he was doing. Thomas was a very special person in her life—though she had never thought to tell him so.

Thomas nodded, a new sparkle coming to his eyes. "I don't have much, but I plan to plant a bit right out there beside the garden plot."

"Is it warm enough to plant the garden yet?" asked Angela.

"I'll get it ready for you—but I'd give it a few more days. I don't like the feel of the wind today. It could blow in another storm."

Angela could smell the stew and quickly rose to check. A look into the pot showed her that it was bubbling. She stirred it again on the way to the serving bowl she had placed on the table. She could hear the coffee boiling, too, but it was Thomas who moved to lift the pot from the hot stove. Without comment he filled their cups and returned the pot to the back of the stove.

"Mrs. Owens was planting her garden yesterday when I went in to town," Angela commented as she placed the empty stew pot on the cupboard and took her chair at the table.

"Mrs. Owens plants a couple times each spring," replied Thomas, lowering himself to his chair. "She always gets caught by frost. 'No patience,' Papa used to say."

Angela smiled. It was true.

Thomas led them in the table grace.

"I'll be patient," Angela said as she lifted her head.

Thomas passed her the stew and waited while she spooned some onto her plate. Angela knew that Thomas was ravenous after a morning in the field, but he would not serve himself before she was served any more than Papa would have cared for himself before looking after Mama.

"When Derek gets home from school have him check that south fence," Thomas said. "I don't want to take any chances on the cows visiting the neighbors. Grass is still in pretty short supply and grazing might look better to them on the other side of the wire."

Angela nodded.

They talked of common things. Farm life. Neighbors.

Needs. They sipped their second cup of coffee, enjoying the flavor and the chance for a rest. Then Thomas lifted his eyes to the wall clock and hoisted himself from his chair.

Angela knew he had given the horses their allotted time to feed and rest and he was ready to resume plowing. She stirred in her chair. She had dishes to do, the wash water to empty, and clothes to iron as soon as the spring breeze had dried the garments hanging on the line. Before she knew it another day would be gone and it would be time for the children to come home from school. They would arrive in a flurry of excitement over the day's events and be looking for a glass of cold milk and a cookie or two and a listening ear as they recounted the day's events.

She watched Thomas lift his cap from the corner peg and leave the kitchen with long strides. "Don't forget about the fence," he called back over his shoulder.

Angela cleared the table and stacked the dishes in the dishpan. She would take care of the wash water first. But when she went out into the yard she found that Thomas had already emptied the tubs. They were hanging in their proper places on the side of the back porch and the washstand was folded and put against the house. *He is very thoughtful,* Angela mused as she turned back toward the kitchen. The tubs were heavy, especially when they were full, and she was thankful the job had already been done.

As she walked toward the kitchen she felt the clothes on the line and removed a few pieces dry enough for ironing. She would get started on that task after doing the dishes.

Chapter Two

Family

"Guess what?" Louise called before she had even opened the kitchen door.

Angela lifted her head from her ironing, her eyes brightening. She always enjoyed this time of the day when the children came bustling into the kitchen, words tumbling over words as they shared the day's adventures. She didn't have a chance to reply before Louise hurried on.

"Marigold likes Derek."

Angela turned her eyes to Derek. The boy said nothing, but a red tinge began to flush his cheeks. His eyes fell.

"Louise," reprimanded Angela gently, "don't tease."

"Well, it's true. Isn't it, Sara? She tried to sit beside him and everything."

Sara nodded, her pigtails bouncing and a mischievous grin lighting her face.

Poor Derek, thought Angela. *So shy—and now this.*

"Lots of girls like Thomas, too," she countered. "I've watched them at church and at picnics. They try to get his attention in all sorts of ways. There's nothing wrong with having friends."

"But," argued Louise, trying to keep her announcement controversial, "Thomas is growed up."

"Grown up," corrected Angela. "Grown up."

"Derek is still just a kid."

"Kids need friends, too," said Angela in Derek's defense.

"Well—not that kind. Not the kind Marigold wants to be. She smiles silly smiles and rolls her eyes and says, 'Oh-h-h,' like that, and all sorts of silly things."

"Derek is not responsible for the way Marigold acts," Angela said firmly. "He is only responsible for himself. Mama always said that true breeding is shown in how we respond to the foolishness of others," she finished, her voice softer.

Louise lowered her eyes, and Angela noticed the stiffness in her shoulders. She had seen such responses before and they concerned her. There was an attitude of resentment there, as though Angela had somehow managed to spoil a bit of Louise's fun.

Angela's eyes clouded as she placed her flatiron back on the stove and added a few sticks of wood to the fire. It was time to change the subject before doing more harm.

"Get your milk from the icebox," she instructed the children. "Louise, you can get the milk and Sara the glasses. Derek, the cookies are in the blue tin."

All three moved to do as bidden. "Get the big glasses," Louise called to Sara. "I'm really thirsty."

"As soon as you have finished, change your school clothes and care for your chores," Angela went on.

There was silence for a few minutes and then Louise lifted her head and stared at Angela.

"Why do you always say that?" she asked.

"Say what?" asked Angela.

" 'Change your school clothes and care for your chores,' " said Louise, mimicking Angela.

"Because it always needs to be done," Angela responded simply.

"Don't you think we know that? We've been doing it ever since—ever since we started off to school—and I'm in fifth grade now."

Panic began to stir in Angela's breast. Louise had never openly challenged her before, and she wasn't sure how to handle it. Nor, for the first time in her life, was she sure how Mama would have handled it. Was there something in her past that would give her direction? She groped around in her memories for a few minutes and came up empty. She could not remember *ever* having challenged Mama, and none of the others were old enough to defy her Mama when—

"That's naughty," Sara was saying to Louise. "We're s'pose to 'bey Angela."

Louise said nothing, but her eyes challenged Angela further.

Derek shuffled uncomfortably. He hated discord.

"She's not our mama," Louise said in a defiant whisper.

"Well—she—she has to take care of us," Derek managed in a weak voice. "And—and you know what Thomas would say if—if he heard you talking sass."

Louise flipped her braids.

"And Thomas is not our papa," she responded, repeating the challenge.

Derek's face paled. Angela was afraid he might burst into tears or flee the room. She moved over to place a hand quickly on his narrow shoulder. She could feel him trembling under his coarse woolen shirt.

"We don't got a mama and papa anymore," cut in Sara insistently. "Angela and Thomas are all we got."

The comment hung in the air for a moment. A sharp pain stabbed Angela's heart when she realized that this fact did not seem to bother Sara to any great degree. She wondered if young Sara could even remember the father and mother she had lost.

"Louise," said Angela as softly as she could, "go to your room, please. We need to have a talk. I will be in just as soon as Derek and Sara have had their milk and cookies."

Dear God, what will I do if she refuses to obey me? Angela wondered, but to her relief, Louise only gave her an angry look and moved toward the bedroom.

Angela tried to calm her trembling soul as she poured the milk. She had an ordeal ahead of her and she wasn't sure how to handle it. None of the children had ever challenged her authority before. What was she to do—and how often in the future might she need to face the same crisis?

Oh, God, she prayed. *Help me with this. What should I do?*

I've noticed—I've noticed little hints of tension—but this—this open defiance—I have no idea—Her voice trembled as she spoke to Derek, "Thomas would like you to check the south fence. He doesn't want the cows getting out. I'll have Louise and Sara help with some of your other chores so you won't be working after dark."

"What do I have to do?" asked Sara.

"Well, you can feed the hens and gather the eggs as usual; then you can help Louise fill the wood box."

"What if Louise doesn't want to?" questioned Sara as she dipped her cookie into her milk.

Angela hesitated. *What if Louise didn't want to?* "Louise is a part of this family," she finally said. "We all must share in the work. I'm afraid she will have to do her share of chores— whether she wants to or not."

Angela delayed her visit to the bedroom as long as she could and then went slowly toward the closed door. She had no idea what she might face when she opened it, and she prayed silently with every step she took. Would Louise still be tossing her blond braids and looking at her with angry eyes? Would she be prostrate on the bed, sobbing for the mother they had lost? Would she have left the room through the opened window and fled to who-knew-where?

But Louise was seated calmly on the chair by the bed reading from her favorite book. She had changed into her chore clothes and her school garments were neatly hung on the pegs on her wall. Her bed was not wrinkled from a bout of crying and her face was not flushed or tear-streaked. She looked quite composed.

"Louise," spoke Angela as she closed the door softly behind her, "I think we need to talk a bit."

Louise nodded.

"Perhaps I do—do tell you over and over again—what I expect you to do. I—I still need to tell Sara. She hasn't—well, hasn't heard it as often as you—and I guess—well, I guess when I am telling one—it is just easier to include all of you."

Louise nodded, no defiance in her eyes now.

"I'm sorry," Angela said softly. "I—I'll try to—to remember

that unless—unless it is a new chore—that you are responsible enough to know—to look after your usual duties."

Louise nodded again.

Angela waited for a moment. She didn't want to spoil the calm, but she knew Louise had to be given further instructions.

"Tonight there are some more things to do," she ventured. "Thomas needs Derek to—to check the fence, so Derek won't have time for his usual chores. That means you and Sara must carry the wood and maybe even feed the pigs."

Angela waited. There was no angry stiffening of Louise's back. She simply nodded.

Angela sighed with relief, tears threatening to spill over. She sat down on the bed near her younger sister and took her hand.

"Louise," she said as gently as she could, "you know that when Mama died she—she asked me to care for all of you. I—I told her I would. Now Mama—Mama felt strongly that caring was—was more than putting food on the table—and seeing that your clothes were washed and mended. Mama wants you—each of us—to grow to be strong, good, dependable. Part of that that growing process comes by sharing chores—and learning obedience. Now I know it won't always be easy to—to have an older sister be your—your authority but—"

Louise stirred on her cushioned seat.

"But that's the way it is," continued Angela. "Not by our choosing, but that's the way it is."

Louise lowered her head, the tears forming in her eyes trickling down her soft cheeks. She sniffed, lifted her eyes, and nodded. That was all. Just a slight nod of her head. But Angela knew that for now it was enough. She gave her sister a hug and stood up.

"Your milk and cookies are on the table," she began, then quickly bit her lip before she followed the statement with what chores needed to be done afterward.

Louise got to her feet and dried her eyes.

She is still such a child, Angela thought as she watched

her. Her heart ached for the young girl.

In typical youthful fashion, Louise gave her big sister a smile, seeming to have already forgotten the battle of a few moments before, and bounded off to the kitchen for her snack.

And don't run, Angela almost called after her. *A lady does not—*

But Louise was not a lady. She was still a little girl of eleven. Playful and careless. And with so very much to learn. "Oh, God," breathed Angela as she sank down onto the bed again and lifted a trembling hand to her face. "How am I ever going to be able to teach them all they need to know? All that Mama would want them to know? Will I ever be able to make a lady out of Louise? Of Sara? Will I be able to teach them about you? Will Thomas be able to fill in for the father Derek needs? Oh, God, we need an awful lot of help."

Chapter Three

Memories

"Something bothering you?"

Angela turned her head to look at Thomas through the soft darkness settling in about them as they sat on the veranda. She had hoped her worries had not shown, but she should have known that Thomas would realize she was anxious about something.

"It's Louise," sighed Angela. "I think she is missing Mama. It's almost as if she misses her more now than—"

Thomas nodded in understanding, then swatted a mosquito that had landed on his bare forearm.

"In what way?" he asked.

"Tonight when I spoke to her about her chores, she—she said I wasn't her mama." Angela couldn't keep the tremor from her voice.

"Did she do her chores?" asked Thomas.

Angela wondered if he was about to waken the young girl out of a sound sleep to make sure she had done her work properly.

"Oh yes. Her fuss didn't last long—then she was sweet as can be. But—well—it just troubles me. What are we going to do if she decides she doesn't want to do our bidding? I mean— if Papa was here—he required obedience with one stern look. But what if—?"

"She hasn't done this before, has she?"

"No. But I'm just scared that it might be the first of many.

She is growing up, you know—and she has always—well—had a mind of her own."

"You want me to talk to her?"

"Oh no."

"Do you want me to punish her? Give her an extra chore or—"

"Oh my, no," cut in Angela quickly. "She doesn't need more punishment. She's already lost her mama."

After a moment of silence, Thomas answered through the spreading darkness, "We have all lost our mama."

"I—I know," Angela said with a trembling voice, "but I think it is harder on the younger ones."

There was another short silence, and Thomas, again, was the one to break it. "It has been three years," he said softly. "They should be sorta—well—getting used to it now."

"That's what frightens me," Angela admitted. "I always—we always thought it would get easier—with the passing of time and all. But it hasn't. I mean, when they were little it was just a case of feeding them and looking after their clothes and—and loving them a lot. Now—now I have a feeling that all those years without Mama to guide them—to show them how to be ladies, to teach them how to treat others, how to show respect and obedience—that's what they've missed, Thomas."

"You've been giving them that," Thomas assured Angela. "Why, at the last church picnic I heard some of the ladies talking about what fine kids they are and what good manners they have and—" Angela was pleased to hear the comment, but she knew that much more than 'please' and 'thank you' was involved in properly raising children.

"They have proper conduct—on the outside. At least I think they have," Angela agreed. "But on the inside? All the things Mama taught—about thinking of others—about not letting little hurts make one into a snob or complainer—about seeing beauty in simple things—about—about so many things. I'm afraid I haven't been getting some of those lessons across to the girls. I—I'm not even sure how Mama did it. I just know that those thoughts—those feelings are there—

deep inside of me—and they came from Mama."

Angela laid a quivering hand over her heart and blinked away tears that wanted to fall. At length she was able to go on.

"I was old enough to understand—to remember those lessons—but I'm afraid Louise and Sara won't remember. Mama was too sick those last months to be able to—to—"

Angela could go no further. Thomas touched her hand briefly in the darkness. They sat silently together, listening to the croaking of the frogs in the pond beyond the barn. An owl hooted into the night. Then a cow bawled somewhere off in the distance and another replied somewhere beyond.

"You're doing a fine job, Angela," Thomas said hoarsely. "I'm proud of the girls and of Derek."

"I am, too," Angela admitted. "But I worry. I want so much for them to grow up to be—to be the children Mama would have been proud of."

"They will," said Thomas with confidence. "They will."

Angela made no reply but her brow still puckered with concern. Would they? Louise was already showing defiance. True, her little bit of fuss hadn't lasted for more than a few minutes, but what would come next? Would she again be telling Angela that she didn't have to accept her authority?

And what of Sara? She was such a carefree, sweet little darling. But she was about as wild and uncontrolled as a prairie mustang. Mama had always wanted her daughters to be little ladies, with clean pinafores, carefully manicured fingernails, neatly braided hair, skirts arranged tidily over properly crossed ankles. Sara never seemed to remember—or care about any of those things, though Angela was sure she had told her about each of them at least a hundred times.

"I do worry about Derek sometimes." Thomas broke in on her thoughts through the darkness.

Angela's head came up quickly. "What do you mean?" she asked. "What's he done? He's never given me a moment's trouble."

"That's just it," responded Thomas thoughtfully. "When I was his age—well, I was giving both Papa and Mama a bit of trouble."

"You—?"

"Don't you remember the number of times I was sent to my room or had to carry extra wood or miss a ball game? Boy, I was always in trouble of some kind."

Angela smiled. It was true. Thomas had been in hot water a good deal of the time.

"Well, Mama and Papa knew how to manage it," Angela said, feeling that it gave strength to her argument. "But how will we—?"

"The same way, I guess," Thomas cut in. "The youngsters need discipline—even if they haven't got a mother or father."

"I'm afraid it's going to be so hard. I mean—I don't mind cooking and cleaning. I think I have done a fair job of that. But, Thomas—I'm not sure I am quite so good at—at mothering."

She could hear his soft chuckle. "Well, you are a mite young to be doing it," he reminded her. "At seventeen most girls aren't married yet—let alone mothers of half-grown kids."

"Yes—and most young men of nineteen aren't responsible for a family of five, either," replied Angela. "You've been running the farm for three years. Well, four really. You had to take over even before Mama—"

Angela stopped. It was too difficult to say the words, even now. She wrapped her hands in her apron and let the conversation become thoughts.

It had all been so strange. So ironic. They had moved west because her mother had not been well and the doctor said that the cooler, clear air of the region might be easier on her lungs. Her father had sold his productive Iowa farm and loaded everything they could take with them in three wagons.

The trip had been a real adventure. Angela still had many memories of it, but the younger children could remember virtually nothing of the move west.

Thomas remembered, of course, because he was older than Angela. And the stories he told about the trip revealed that, to him, it had been an adventure of a lifetime.

They had found new land—a new life—and their father

had set about building a farm again. He put all his strength
and energy into building the house and barns. Into erecting
straight, even fences. Into plowing land to prepare it for seed.
Into clearing rock and planting a windbreak.

The farm soon responded, taking on the well-cared-for look
of their previous one. Her father was a good farmer, a hard-
working man, and soon the farm was the most productive,
most attractive one in the area.

Her mother's health did improve—at least for a while. She
seemed to breathe more easily, seemed to have more energy
in her slight frame. And then a winter cold put her back in
bed and the family watched as she gradually lost ground in
her long fight for health. But even from her bed she continued
to guide her family. Angela remembered the long talks, the
careful instructions. Looking back she realized now that her
mother had been grooming her for the task ahead, but Angela
had not been aware of it at the time. It was so easy for her to
pretend that her mother would soon be well again, that things
would return to normal.

But it was their strong, healthy father who left them first.
An aneurysm, the doctor had said, shaking his head sadly.
"We never know when they might strike—or whom. Some-
times they pick the most unlikely."

So it was Thomas who first had to shoulder the responsibilities of an adult. Thomas—at age sixteen—took over all the
farm duties.

Their father had taught him well. He was a hard worker,
and a built-in pride drove him to try to maintain things just
as his father had always done. The farm had repaid him.
Though no one could have thought of them as wealthy, they
had never been in want.

Seven short months later, their mother also slipped away
from them. At the last Angela had the feeling that Mama was
almost eager to join her husband, though she did put up a
long, hard fight to live for the sake of her children. The days
before her passing were spent in long talks whenever Angela's
duties allowed a little free time. The three younger children
were all in school. Angela envied them at first. She'd had to

give up classes to help at home. Her mother had sensed how she felt and made sure to provide books so Angela could continue learning. But as her mother's condition worsened, Angela had no time for reading or studying.

And then her mother was gone. She was laid to rest beside their father on the green knoll by the little church. Thomas and Angela were now solely responsible for their three siblings. They never questioned their lot. There was a task to be done and they put their time and attention into doing it.

———

Angela stirred. The spring evening was getting cool, and she knew they should go in. Tomorrow would be another long day. She still felt an uneasiness within her. Now she was not only worried about Louise and Sara, Thomas had unwittingly added Derek to her list of concerns.

"About Derek," she said slowly, "what exactly are you worried about?"

"Well, he's just so—so quiet. He never speaks what's on his mind. I'm just afraid he might be dwelling more on Pa— or Mama—being gone than we realize."

Angela had not thought of that before. It was true that Derek was quiet—pensive. He was always most cooperative, but perhaps that was not always a true sign of how he was feeling.

"Maybe he needs more boy fun," suggested Angela. "Remember when you were his age? You were always off fishing. Or playing ball. Or chasing frogs or—or hunting bird nests or something."

Thomas nodded.

"Well, Derek never does any of those things."

"I know," said Thomas. "He's more like a little old man than a boy."

Angela had never seen it that way before. Now she realized Thomas was right.

"What can we do?" she wondered out loud.

"I've been thinking. Maybe I should take him fishing—or something."

Angela unfolded her tense hands and reached out to touch Thomas's sleeve.

"That's a wonderful idea!" she exclaimed. "When?"

"Well, I don't know—exactly. I've got to get the crop in and then—"

"Thomas, I don't think you should wait. Not until you have everything done. You know how it is. On a farm there is always something that needs doing. You'll never find the time if you wait for it all to be done."

"Well, I can't just up and leave the work while I run off to—"

"Why? Why not? The kids are more important than anything else. I know that's what Mama would say. She would want you to go. At least for a couple of days—even an afternoon if that's all you can manage. We need to be—to be putting first things first. I mean—what good is the farm if—?"

"Maybe I can take an afternoon," said Thomas.

"This Saturday," Angela prompted, the idea filling her with excitement. She was sure Derek would be pleased.

"This Saturday? I was planning to plow up your garden Saturday afternoon," replied Thomas.

"It can wait. Like you said, there's no reason to get impatient."

"This Saturday then. Hope the weather stays good. No fun fishing in the rain."

Nothing much had changed. There was still the problem of responsibility. Angela still faced the need for mothering a brother and two sisters. But somehow just this one small planned action lifted the anxiety from her heart. At least they were planning. They were trying to do more than just feed and clothe their siblings. And it wasn't her alone. She had Thomas to help her, to share the responsibilities. For some reason her load had lifted as she stood and turned back to the lighted kitchen.

"I must take more time to do things with the girls," she said, more to herself than to Thomas as he held the door open for her. "All I have been doing is handing out orders. Do this. Don't do that. They need time to be children."

"Children, yes," agreed Thomas, "but responsible children."

"That's what scares me. It is my job to make sure that's what they are."

"You're doing fine."

"But I need to—to find ways to teach them. Encourage them. Just like Mama did with me."

Thomas let a hand drop to her shoulder. "Don't be too hard on yourself, Angie," he cautioned. "Don't set the standards impossibly high. You're human, too, you know."

Angela was very aware of that as she picked up the lamp to light her way to her bedroom. Thomas had turned to bolt the door behind them. In the semidarkness he looked like her pa standing there. She had never noticed the likeness before. Her pa would be so proud. So proud of his son. But Thomas had been almost raised before they had lost their parents. If only—if only she could bring the others up to deserve family pride, too. If only they would grow up to be responsible members of society. If only they grew up to love God and belong to His family . . .

Chapter Four

Neighbors

There had been disagreement among the people in the community as to what should be done with the Peterson children when they lost their parents. The Blackwells, to the north of the Peterson farm, had never been blessed with a family of their own, but that did not prevent Mrs. Blackwell from expressing very decided opinions about the children.

"They need caring for," she stated, "by adults who are responsible." She suggested that the children be divided among district families and that she and her husband take Sara and Derek. When Thomas stated firmly that they had no intention of parcelling the children out here and there, Mrs. Blackwell changed her mind as to what should be done.

"Iffen they are to be responsible citizens," she maintained, "then they need to do their own caring. I don't plan to be a caterin' to 'em."

And she didn't.

"No use fussin' over 'em. They've made them their jam. Now let 'em eat it."

But Mr. Blackwell apparently didn't share his wife's view. On occasion he was seen delivering a sack of seed potatoes to the Petersons or making sure they had enough coal in the bin.

The Petersons' closest neighbor was a sour man who lived on his own. From outward appearances, he may not even have known the Peterson family existed, or that they were left on their own. He was not old—nor was he young. His face was

31

weathered from being outdoors riding herd on his cattle or supervising maintenance and repairs on his property. He was not popular in the neighborhood, but no one spoke of it much. He was far too rich and powerful for anyone to risk getting on his bad side. Only his hired hand, Charlie, who acted as foreman of the spread, seemed able to get along with the crusty Mr. Stratton. Angela wondered if perhaps it was because Charlie was the only one who had known his boss long enough to be aware of the circumstances that had shaped him.

"Oh, he ain't so bad as all thet," Charlie would say. "He barks a lot, but I ain't seen him bite yet."

Charlie, in his own quiet way, was more help to the Peterson youngsters than anyone else in the neighborhood. In the evenings, after completing his daily rounds, he would slip over to their house. Sometimes he brought things from town, sometimes he gave hints as to how Thomas should plant or plow. Sometimes he just came to chat and to see that everything was going all right. Those first years would have been awfully difficult without Charlie.

The pastor was supportive—but he was a very busy man. He shouldered the burdens of the congregation as well as his own young family.

The Reverend Merrifield had lost his first wife and then married again, a fine widow with a family of her own. The new marriage had given them a family of eight. His Roger, Ernest, and Lucy, and her Peter, Pauline, and Perry. To that number had been added little Priscilla and Pearl. In addition to the confusion of so many in one household, there was also a bit of friction between the oldest sons. One of the conflicts, unknown to Angela, involved her. Both boys spent a good deal of time lobbying for position to get a bit of her attention. Roger was eighteen and Peter seventeen. Most folks thought they should have been out on their own by now, providing the family with income, but they lived at home, doing only odd jobs here and there as they were able to find them in town.

There were families in the church who expressed concern about the Petersons. The Conroys, who were neighboring farmers to the west, spoke frequently about their intentions to give a hand here and there. Occasionally they did, but their own field work and gardens took so much time that little was left for the Petersons. They did, however, faithfully remember the children in their daily prayers. The Conroys had a family of their own to consider. Hazel, nineteen, was a friendly enough girl, but being older than Angela, she had always seemed to feel a bit superior as well, and now that she was making preparations for her coming marriage, she acted queenly indeed. Roberta was Angela's age and might have been a real companion had she not been severely handicapped because of a serious case of measles at age three. Angela would gladly have offered her friendship, but Roberta preferred to play with young children. Ingrid and Bertha Conroy were good friends of Louise and Sara, wanting to spend more time at one another's houses than their own.

The Sommerses also attended the local church, and their daughter, Trudie, was Angela's age. It was accepted by the church members that Trudie was Angela's best friend, but the truth was, Angela was not sure about Trudie. At times Trudie gushed and fussed, at other times she seemed to pass Angela by without even a nod of acknowledgement. Trudie tended to be peacock-proud, tossing her reddish mane with snobbish abandon, and about as flighty as a barn swallow. She was always getting herself into some kind of tizzy about something. But the church folk were often heard to say with deep feeling, "It's so nice that Angela has Trudie."

Angela tried to be friendly to Trudie. After all, she was the only girl her own age with whom to associate. And Angela was in need of an understanding companion. Yet she hesitated to share anything important with Trudie. She was never sure that her secret thoughts or feelings would be kept secret for long.

The Sommerses had three other children. Claude, thirteen, was Derek's age, and was kind and considerate. Angela regarded Claude as one of the finest young boys she knew and was happy to encourage friendship between him and her little brother. But for reasons Angela could not determine, Derek held himself back from forming close friendships.

Then there were Baxter, nine, and Wylie, eight. Sara was constantly being teased and taunted by the school children about one or the other, so Baxter and Wylie were off limits as a topic of conversation in the Peterson household.

The dearest and closest friends of the Peterson family were the Andrewses. Mr. Andrews operated the town mercantile, the store where Angela did the family shopping. He was a soft-spoken man, as good at living out his religion as declaring it. There were few people who could have found anything disparaging to say about Mr. Andrews—they would have needed to embellish it with untruths. He was not interfering, but each member of the Peterson family knew that if ever a need arose, Mr. Andrews was the man to whom they should go.

Mrs. Andrews was a motherly woman who had little to say but whose smile welcomed everyone. And her instincts seemed always to be right. She passed out cookies and hugs with abandon. Even Thomas, big and strapping as he was, accepted his share, and Angela felt that some of her days were made endurable because of the embrace of the kind woman.

The Andrews family had not escaped sorrow. Their daughter Emma had been Angela's best friend before the girl had drowned in a tragic accident when the girls were nine. Perhaps that was another reason Mrs. Andrews used any occasion to hold Angela close for a moment.

There were three others in the family. Frankie, their youngest, was nine, and Agnes a grown-up twelve, but of the Andrews family it was Thane who was the dearest friend of the Petersons.

Thane was the same age as Thomas, and the two boys were as close as brothers. They had spent much of their earlier years fishing or hiking together. Angela remembered many times they had stayed at the other's house. It was Thane with Thomas or Thomas with Thane. But Karl Peterson's sudden death changed that greatly. Thomas was no longer free to be a carefree lad, off on nature hikes or overnight campouts. In that instant he became a farmer, responsible for the welfare of a family. So now it was up to Thane to come their way— and he did—often—bringing sacks of penny candy, a bright red "spinner" for fishing, or new hair ribbons for the girls tucked in his pocket.

And so life went on for the Peterson children, even though some days were heavy with sorrow and others weighted with responsibility. Although the neighbors occasionally reached out a loving or helping hand, for the most part the young people were assumed to be capable of caring for themselves.

Chapter Five

Party

"Angela, wait."

Angela recognized the voice of Trudie Sommers. She turned and pushed back her bonnet to wait for her friend.

The girl was running toward Angela, skirts and ribbons flying out behind her.

"Don't run," called Angela. "It's too hot. I'll wait."

Trudie slowed to a walk, but at a brisk, excited pace.

Angela leaned over and put her parcel of groceries on the grass. Then she straightened again and brushed curls of blond hair from her face.

"I thought I'd missed you," gasped Trudie, finally reaching Angela. "Mrs. Layton said you would be halfway home."

Angela laughed. "I should have been—but I stopped to see the new Willis baby."

"Isn't she a darling?" said Trudie somewhat distractedly.

" 'She' is a 'he,' " Angela smiled.

"Oh yes, well," Trudie replied, then quickly changed the subject. "I wanted to let you know that I am having a party on Saturday night."

"A party?" Angela couldn't remember when she had last been to a party.

"I'd like you to come," Trudie hurried to say.

"What kind of a party?" asked Angela.

"Just some friends. We'll play party games and—and eat," she laughed.

It sounded wonderful to Angela. With all her heart she wished she could go.

"I'd love to but—"

"No buts," cut in Trudie. "Everyone thinks you need to get out and have a little fun. You're only seventeen, you know. Not seventy."

"Yes, but—" Angela stopped. Trudie was right. She did need a little fun. She wondered if she even knew how to have fun anymore.

"I'll see if Thomas will stay with the kids," she said, but then noticed the disappointed expression on Trudie's face.

"I was hoping Thomas would be able to come, too," Trudie said.

Angela was quick to sense the circumstances. Perhaps Thomas was the real target of the invitation. She had seen a number of young women from town watching Thomas. Some were quite bold in their nods and smiles. Angela felt sure that her mama would not have approved of such forwardness.

"I'll see," Angela promised. "I'll talk it over with Thomas."

Trudie's lips formed a smile again. "Good," she responded. "I'll be expecting you." She turned to leave, and Angela hoisted the heavy package and headed toward home.

All the way Angela thought about the invitation. She couldn't remember the last time she and Thomas had been to a party. She wondered if Thomas would accept. He had already taken one afternoon from his work to go fishing with Derek.

"I wonder if Thomas will agree," mused Angela. "And if he does, what will we do with the children?"

The rest of the day was busy for Angela. She forgot about the party until after the children were tucked into bed for the night. As she and Thomas spent a few minutes on the veranda before retiring, she remembered the invitation.

"Oh, I 'most forgot," Angela began. "We had an invitation to a party today."

Thomas laughed.

"It's Saturday night. Just neighborhood friends. Games and food."

Thomas chuckled again. "What makes folks think we have time for partying?" he asked.

"It would be fun to go," Angela ventured.

"You can go if you want to," Thomas said quickly.

"You won't go?"

"I'm not much into partying," he replied.

"How do you know?" asked Angela. "I don't remember you trying it."

Thomas just shrugged.

"Trudie said—" Angela saw Thomas's head lift and knew he was waiting for her to go on.

"Trudie said that she hoped you would be able to come, too."

Thomas shrugged again, but Angela noticed something different about the movement. He was no longer laughing. He seemed to be considering the invitation.

"Will you?" asked Angela.

"Might not hurt—this once," responded Thomas lightly.

"What will we do with the kids?"

Thomas looked surprised at the mention of the children. After a few moments of thought he responded. "Guess it wouldn't hurt none for them to stay alone for a few hours. After all, they aren't babies anymore. You and I were almost running things by the time we were their age."

The suggestion troubled Angela. She found it hard to believe that the children were old enough to be left alone. Still, she must not coddle them, she reasoned. Papa had always been one to give added responsibility as age increased.

"Maybe so—if we aren't gone too long," she said hesitantly.

And so it was decided that Thomas and Angela would accept the invitation to the Sommerses' party. They gave careful instructions to the three children about what would be expected of them "on their own."

"Why can't I go?" fussed Louise.

"The party is for—for older people," responded Angela, trying to keep her voice firm yet gentle.

"Well, I don't think it's fair," Louise continued, but a stern look from Thomas made her fall silent.

"I'll have a party for some of your friends," Angela put in quickly. "I promise. We'll plan it together."

"When?" asked Louise.

"Just as soon as the garden is planted," replied Angela.

"Sure—you just want me to help with the garden," Louise accused.

"You always help with the garden," Angela returned evenly.

"Well, you want me to do more. More than my rightful share. You think that I'll—"

"Louise," said Thomas sternly, and Louise left the room before saying anymore.

Angela looked at Thomas. "Let her go," she whispered. "She's having a hard time growing up. I—I just don't know quite how to help her."

When the night of the party arrived Angela held her breath in case Thomas backed out at the last minute, but he didn't. Angela noticed his fussing over his shoes and hair. He spent more time before the kitchen basin slicking down his wayward cowlick than Angela spent pinning up her own tresses.

Angela tried not to let him see that she was noticing his lengthy grooming, but she did wonder about it.

They walked the road together and cut across the neighbors' field to speed their progress. Thomas had a hard time slowing his stride to accommodate his sister. Angela had never seen him so eager before.

Perhaps he has been missing fun, she reasoned, wondering why he had never shared with her how he felt.

Trudie met them at the gate. She reached a hand to Angela, but it was Thomas who got her full attention.

"I'm so glad you could come," she said, her voice soft and warm, and Angela felt a funny little prick of fear running up her spine.

Trudie out to win Thomas? Could it be? *It was Thomas she wanted all along,* Angela suddenly realized. *She didn't care about me at all. She just wanted me to get Thomas here.*

Angela felt betrayed. Rejected. And terribly annoyed with Trudie—even with Thomas. Thomas was smiling back at Trudie. He even allowed her to take his arm and draw him toward the circle of neighborhood friends. Angela seemed to have been forgotten. It occurred to her that she could just hoist her skirts above the dust of the roadway and make her way directly back home. She was about to do so when she felt someone take hold of her arm. She was hardly in the mood to be civil, much less friendly. Who else besides Trudie might treat her as if she were some mindless dolt—like Thomas suddenly seemed to have become?

"Glad you could come," said a voice at her side, and Angela recognized it immediately. *It's just Thane,* she thought, relieved.

"Thank you," she said, but her troubled thoughts made it difficult to control her voice.

She didn't try to pull her arm away, though. If Thomas wasn't planning to be with her it would be a comfort to have Thane nearby.

Her eyes still followed Trudie and Thomas. Trudie's silly laugh floated across the yard, and she was hanging on to Thomas's arm as though her life depended on it. The part that bothered Angela was that Thomas did not seem to object.

What if Trudie was successful in wooing Thomas? Who would run the farm? Help raise the children? Angela cast a nervous look at the bubbling girl. Surely Thomas would see through the ploy, would let Trudie know in no uncertain terms that he was not interested.

But Thomas was still smiling at Trudie and responding to her playful glances with animated conversation.

Thane carefully guided Angela toward a small group of young people. Some of them were from church, and before Angela had time to think further about her concerns, she was included in the circle and made to feel welcome. Now and then throughout the evening she stole a glance at Thomas. Each time, Trudie was not far from his side. Angela tried to push aside the nagging fear. Thomas belonged to the family. He

was hers. Had always been hers. They had been together ever
since their pa and ma had left them. They bolstered each other,
encouraged each other, cheered each other. If she should lose
Thomas, she wasn't sure she would be able to carry on.

"Care for a sandwich?" Thane was asking.

Angela's thoughts jerked back to the moment and she tried
to smile.

"I'm really not very hungry," she managed, shaking her
head.

Thane accepted her reply and took a seat beside her. He
passed her the sandwich he had just offered her and winked.
"If you don't want it, would you mind holding it for me until
I'm done with this one?" he asked.

Angela couldn't help but smile. She held the sandwich as
she watched the group of merrymakers before her, then took
a bite to Thane's approving nod. Everyone seemed to be having
such fun. For a moment she felt cheated that she wasn't able
to wholeheartedly join them. But her thoughts kept going
back to Thomas, then to the children at home.

What am I doing here? she asked herself. *These people don't
have a care in the world. Not one of them knows what it's like
to have full responsibility for a family. I shouldn't be partying.
I have long since forgotten how.*

Thane was speaking to her. It took a moment for the meaning to make sense to her. Could he get her anything? He was
going to get another sandwich "since you have eaten mine,"
he teased. As she shook her head, she noticed the concern in
his eyes.

"Something wrong?" he asked. "You're a million miles
away."

Angela managed a smile and stirred restlessly on her log
seat. "I guess I'm just not much good at partying," she replied.
"I—I keep thinking of the kids at home."

"Want me to walk you back?" he asked. "No need for ol'
Tom to leave yet. He seems to be having himself a great time."

Angela could hear the chuckle in Thane's voice. He didn't
seem to have any problem with the way Thomas was carrying
on.

" 'Ol' Tom,' " she said with emphasis, "should remember that he needs to be up early in the morning to have the chores done in time for church."

"I reckon Tom won't be forgetting that," replied Thane easily. "Never known him to miss church—or chores—yet."

Thane was the only one who ever called her brother Tom. Angela didn't know why. Everyone else called Thomas by his given name. Why Thane chose not to use it—and why Thomas never seemed to object—she had no idea.

Angela really did want to go, yet she hated to be the one to break up the party.

"Well," she said, "it has been fun—but all good things must end, they say." She tried to sound light and carefree like the others about her.

"You're really going now?" asked Thane.

"I think we should. We have been gone long enough. Would you mind telling Thomas that I'm ready to go?"

Thane nodded his head and went to speak to him. Angela was sure that Thomas, when he heard she was leaving the party, would quickly get her wrap and escort her home.

But it didn't happen that way. Thomas looked her direction for a moment, gave her a careless wave of his hand, then spoke to Thane again.

It was Thane who arrived with her wrap. Thomas was still chatting with a group of young people. Trudie was near him, though not leaning on his arm as she had been so often during the evening.

"Ready?" asked Thane as he settled the wrap about her shoulders.

Angela allowed Thane to lead her from the group. Laughter followed them as they walked down the lane, and Angela wondered how much longer the party would continue.

"Good thing there is a full moon," Thane observed. "It's easier to see the way."

"Oh, I expect that Trudie calculated well," Angela responded moodily. "She would have been sure to order a full moon."

Thane seemed puzzled by her comment but made no reply.

After a few attempts at light conversation, Thane let Angela walk in silence. Occasionally he reached out a hand to help her over some rough ground. She accepted without protest. She was almost as used to Thane as to Thomas. He had always been Thomas's best friend. He spent almost as much time at their house as did her own family. He was as comfortable to be with as Derek. Angela did not pay much attention one way or the other.

But Thane knew her well.

"You're angry about something," he stated when they reached the porch. "Not just worried about the kids—but angry. What happened?"

Angela's chin began to quiver in spite of her attempt to still it.

"Did you see Trudie?" she hissed, squaring her shoulders. "She was—was hanging on to Thomas like—like she owned him."

Thane's answer came with a soft chuckle. "Maybe she would like to."

"Well, she'd better—better back off."

"Why?" Thane asked mildly. "I didn't see Tom objecting."

"Well, he should have. We—we need him here—with us. He—he isn't—"

"Wait a minute," said Thane, taking Angela by the shoulders. "Do I hear you right? Are you saying that you expect ol' Tom to—to just lay life aside and give all of his years to you?"

"Not me," choked Angela. "Not me. The kids need—"

"Angela," Thane broke in seriously, "there might come a day when Tom will choose a life of his own. He deserves that. He has already postponed his own dreams. Is it right to expect him to just forget about all of that—forever?"

Angela shivered. She wanted to lay her head against Thane's shoulder and let the tears fall, but she didn't.

"*I*—I have to," she told him, her voice trembling.

There was silence for a moment; then Thane answered slowly.

"For now," he said. "For now. But may God grant that it might not always be so."

He kissed her forehead gently, and quietly slipped into the night. Angela watched him retreat until he was lost in the shadows; then she turned to the door. Too many emotions were fighting for her attention. She was still angry with Trudie—and with Thomas, though Thane was right. Thomas deserved a life of his own. But what about the children? Who would care for them if Thomas left? And who would share her burden? And what had Thane meant? It would be years before the children were grown and on their own. Angela had no thoughts for anything but the task that still lay ahead of her. She had to raise them properly—for Mama.

Chapter Six

The Game

Angela did not rest well. Thoughts of Thomas deserting the family kept spinning in her head. When she finally fell into a restless sleep, she dreamed she had been split in two and one side was arguing ferociously with the other.

"He can't leave us for some—some pretty face."

"He deserves a chance for a life of his own."

"But we need him far more than she does."

"What if he's not happy here? Do you still think he should stay?"

"We need him. We need him" seemed to be the endless refrain. Angela awoke in a sweat, heart pounding. She wasn't sure which of the two sides had been the real Angela—or maybe they both were.

She was pale and withdrawn as she prepared the morning porridge. The children, in their usual blustery fashion, did not seem to notice that anything was bothering her, which Angela was thankful for. She did feel Derek's eyes upon her once or twice, but he asked no questions.

Thomas seemed even brighter than usual. He whistled his way in from milking the cows and teased the youngsters at the breakfast table.

"Did you have fun at the party?" asked Sara brightly. She tossed back her curls that Angela had formed to go with her Sunday frock.

Thomas answered enthusiastically, "Sure did."

47

"What did you do?" Sara asked next.

Thomas tipped his head to one side as though thinking deeply. "Funny thing," he observed at last. "I don't recall doing much of anything."

"Aw, Thomas. Tell us. Don't be mean," pleaded Sara.

Louise was sitting silently by, picking little bites from her toast and eating them one by one. She still was cross that she hadn't been allowed to attend the party.

Derek seemed totally oblivious to the conversation, as though he were sitting all alone at the breakfast table.

Angela was not pleased with the discussion. She wanted, with all her heart, to blurt out that Thomas had spent the entire evening making a fool of himself in the company of Trudie Sommers. But even as the accusation formed in her mind she knew it was unfair. Thomas had been mannerly and proper. He had simply been a young man enjoying an evening with friends. Nobody, not even Papa or Mama, would have faulted Thomas on his behavior. No one, that is, but his frightened sister.

"C'mon," Sara coaxed. "Tell us what it was like."

"Well, let's see," began Thomas, more serious now. "We played a few games. We talked a lot. We sang a few songs."

Angela's eyes widened. There had been no singing while she was there. She loved to sing. She might have enjoyed the party more if she had participated in the songfest.

Thomas hesitated for just a moment. His eyes lifted to meet Angela's.

"That was after Angela had come home to check on you. She couldn't really enjoy the party for worrying that you were all right. We all missed her soprano in the singing. Several people asked about her."

Angela turned back to the stove. She felt cheated. No one had told her they were planning to sing.

"What else?" asked Sara.

Louise had quit picking at her toast and was listening, but Derek still had not joined the conversation.

"Well—we ate. We ate lots. There was popcorn and gingerbread and chocolate cake with some kind of crispy stuff on top. Angela, you should ask Trudie for that recipe. It was good. Um-m-m," said Thomas, giving his head a shake for emphasis.

Angela had no intention of asking Trudie Sommers for anything. Besides, if things went as Trudie was planning, Thomas could be eating the famous chocolate cake with crispy stuff on top for the rest of his life, Angela reasoned.

"Louise," she said almost sternly, "I believe it is your turn to wash the breakfast dishes. Sara, you dry. And Derek," her voice softened automatically, "I need another block of ice from the ice house."

She saw Derek's nod. He shoved the rest of his toast into his mouth, emptied his milk glass and rose from the table.

Angela was about to remind him to excuse himself when his eyes met hers for just a moment. She thought she saw pain in them. She closed her lips on the words and looked away. She could not bear to gaze so openly into the boy's anguished soul.

As the door shut behind Derek, Angela's attention was caught by Thomas's words.

"And Trudie says we should get together more often." Thomas was continuing his report.

With an angry flip of her hand, Angela dropped the roast into the pot with a loud noise. "I'll just bet she did," she said under her breath, but no one seemed to notice her anger.

"Well, I suppose the others might have another party—but me—I told her I appreciated the offer but I had work that needed doing."

Angela wondered if she heard disappointment in Thomas's voice. A feeling of sympathy tugged at her heart. She could not understand herself. How could she feel angry at Thomas one minute and sorry for him the next? She was so mixed up. She hoped with all her heart that the church service would help her get her thoughts untangled.

———

Angela returned from church having regained a measure of serenity. She still felt concern about rearing her siblings. She still felt a quiver of fear that Thomas might leave them for a life of his own, but she had balanced all of that with the fact that God did truly care about the Peterson family. Surely she didn't bear the burden of their welfare alone.

I must remember that, she chastised herself. If there ever was a lesson Mama emphasized it was that God loves them and would care for them. They only needed to trust Him.

The conversation around the dinner table that noon was of the usual sort. They spoke of the things they had heard that morning. They shared little stories about friends. Even Louise laughed at Thomas's silly jokes and joined in plans of "we should" or "could we?"

In fact, it seemed to Angela that things were back to normal again, and she began to wonder why she had allowed herself to get into such a stew.

Their talk turned to childhood remembrances.

"Remember," she joined in, "when Mama fixed us that little picnic and we ate it out in the yard under the bed sheets?"

Thomas nodded, his eyes sparkling with merriment at the memory, but three pairs of eyes looked blank.

"She pinned the sheets up to the clothesline," explained Thomas, "and then Pooch, that big oaf of a dog, came tearing around the corner of the house, afraid of the old sow or something, and ran smack into the side of it. It came down off the line and wrapped all around him and he ran off yapping, with that sheet flapping out behind him, like he thought the world was coming to an end."

Angela and Thomas laughed until their sides ached.

"And remember the time Mama made those cookies with the great big eyes and funny looks?" Thomas added. "Sad faces, happy faces, frowning faces, surprised faces. Then she put them on a plate and offered each of us one. We all picked a happy face. Remember? And then she said, 'Oh, look. You have all chosen a happy face. I guess everyone prefers a face that is happy. No one wants the sad or angry face. Let's change the rest.' And she did. Then she let us eat them."

Angela nodded. Her mama had been so skillful at getting across simple lessons. If only Angela knew how to do it.

"And remember the time she walked with us to the creek to show us—"

"Mama walked?" cut in Sara, her eyes big with wonder. Both Angela and Thomas turned to look at her.

"What do you mean?" asked Angela.

"I didn't know Mama could walk."

"Of course she could walk."

"All I 'member is her being in bed or sometimes in a chair," continued Sara.

Tears came to Angela's eyes. She had worried that the younger children were forgetting their mother—had not had as many years to glean memories as she and Thomas had enjoyed. But she had not realized just how much they had been denied.

"You don't remember?" she asked.

Sara answered by shaking her head.

"You don't remember having Mama in the kitchen fixing after-school snacks? You don't remember the walks through her garden? You don't remember taking her hand to see the new calf?"

With each question Sara continued shaking her head.

"I remember a little bit," broke in Louise. "I remember the color of her hair. I even remember Papa calling it 'spun gold.' I remember her apron with the big pockets. And I remember one time when I scratched my knee and she fixed it—then she rocked me and sang me a song—about little birdies or something. I forget that part."

Angela was disturbed that her sisters had so few memories of their wonderful mother. No wonder it was so difficult for her to pass along to them all the lessons of proper conduct and correct attitudes. There was no base there, built solidly by their mama.

"Do you remember Mama?" Angela asked, turning to look at Derek. The boy did not lift his eyes from his plate but nodded slightly. Angela saw him swallow. Her eyes misted as she wondered just what memories Derek had tucked away in his heart.

Angela blinked away the tears and responded quickly lest her emotions would overcome her, "Well, it is important for each of us to remember Mama and Papa. If you don't remem-

ber much about them, Thomas and I—and Derek—are going
to have to share our memories. From now on we'll play a little
game and the three of us will share memories about what they
did—what they said—what they were like—so all of us will
know them and have memories."

Sara clapped her hands, her eyes shining. She approved of
the game. Louise nodded her head.

"Thomas, you start," Angela encouraged.

"Well, let's see. Where do I start? There are so many
things."

"Wait," said Angela, jumping up from the table. "Let's
write down each one—then we won't be getting mixed-up and
telling the same ones over and over. And later we can read
them."

Angela returned with a sheet of paper and a pencil.

"The next time I'm in town I'll buy a proper book. For now
this will do."

"Let's call it our Memory Book," put in Sara excitedly.

"And we could divide it into how they looked, what they
did, and what they said," Louise offered, adding, "That way,
Sara and I will get to say something, too."

"Great idea," Angela agreed. "Instead of Thomas going
first, you start, Sara."

Sara puckered her brow and thought deeply. "Well," she
said at last, "I 'member Mama in her bed with a blue blanket
tucked up close around her chin. I thought she was sleeping,
but when I tiptoed in she reached out her hand to me—and
smiled."

Angela swallowed the lump in her throat. She knew from
Sara's account that the incident had happened shortly before
their mother left them. Angela wrote quickly, for she knew
Louise was anxious for her turn.

"I remember," began Louise, "Mama sitting in her chair,
by the fireplace. And she was knitting me mittens. Red ones.
Remember? They were my very favorites—but I lost one and—
I don't know what happened to the other one."

"I guess you lost them both, huh?" teased Thomas.

"I did not. I just lost one," insisted Louise.

"Derek?" encouraged Angela.

Derek fidgeted with his fork, his eyes downcast. He swallowed a few times and eventually spoke. His voice was low and strained, as though speaking was difficult for him.

"I remember Mama baking pie" was all he said.

Angela struggled with the few words. She found it difficult to control her emotions. Poor Derek. He was suffering far more deeply than she had ever known.

"Thomas, now you," Angela managed to say.

"Well, I'm going to share a memory of Papa," said Thomas. "I remember how big Papa was." Thomas stretched his hand in the air to emphasize his point. "I only reached about to the top of his boots—or that's the way it seemed to me. I was so proud when I got as high as his pockets. He used to tuck penny candies in them when he went to town. I remember when I could reach candies on my own."

Angela wrote hurriedly, pressed to keep up with Thomas.

"Your turn. Your turn," her family finally was shouting.

Angela chose to share one of Mama's simple lessons.

"I remember one day when I didn't want to do the washing," she began slowly. "There were lots of grimy clothes. Piles and piles, it seemed, and I thought I would never finish the wash. Mama said, 'Angela, never let your task become a drudge. You are special. You are unique. No matter what your duty, no matter how distasteful you might find it, inside you can be whatever you decide to be. Outside, your hands might be soiled with daily toil—inside, your soul and spirit can be refined and elegant. You can be just as much a lady leaning over a tub of hot, sudsy water scrubbing farm-dirty socks as you can sitting on a velvet cushion, fanning yourself with a silk and ivory fan.' "

"What did she mean?" whispered Sara.

"Well," responded Angela, "I think she was trying to tell us that work is necessary—but it is honorable. It is what you are—deep inside—not what you do that is important."

"You mean," asked Sara, "I can pretend to be a grand lady while I'm washing the dishes?"

"You don't have to pretend," answered Angela. "You can actually be one."

Chapter Seven

Growing

Angela was pleased with the children's excitement over the memory game. Sunday after Sunday they exchanged their stories. With their memories refreshed by the discussions, Louise and Sara were surprised at how many events even they could remember. And Derek always added his brief account.

"Derek still isn't saying much in our game time, is he?" Thomas mentioned one evening as he and Angela sat on the porch together.

"Just a line—a brief sentence," Angela responded. "I hadn't realized how—how many deep hurts must be buried inside him."

"I guess he was right at the age where he needed Papa and Mama the most. And we—you and I—were so busy trying to keep body and soul together that we missed seeing what it was doing to him."

"Poor soul," sighed Angela. "Thomas, do you think we are doing enough?"

Thomas pondered the question. "I don't know," he said at last. "I just don't know. But I'm not sure what else we can do."

"Do you think the minister might be able to help him?"

"Maybe. I just don't know."

"He is so withdrawn—yet so strangely sweet. It's as though—as though he lives in fear of—of causing someone pain or something. He tries so hard to be good. Yet he—he seems so reluctant to even talk about the folks. I'm not sure he even likes our game—though there have been times when I've thought I have seen some light in his eyes at a memory we have discussed."

"Well, for now I guess we'll just continue as we are. I think—I think maybe he is enjoying the company of other boys more. I see him at church joining the group of fellows outside after the service. He didn't use to do that."

"At least he responds now, a little anyway. Though he never initiates a friendship, that's encouraging."

Thomas was about to make another comment when their attention was drawn to a horse and rider coming down the lane.

"It's Thane," announced Thomas, rising from his chair to wave a welcome.

"He hasn't been out for a while," responded Angela.

"His pa has been working him pretty hard in the store. He says he hardly has time to take a Saturday night bath," Thomas laughed.

"I'd better get something ready to eat," Angela said as she stood up. "He's always hungry."

Thomas laughed again, but he didn't argue with her observation.

Angela left for the kitchen as Thomas descended the porch steps to greet their visitor.

Angela heard the voices and the laughter as she stirred lemonade and placed cookies on a plate. Then the voices lowered as though the topic of conversation had become more serious. She stepped out onto the porch in time to hear Thomas ask, "When did it happen?"

"Almost a week ago. Word didn't get out very soon—even though Doc knew about it. Guess Charlie asked him to keep it quiet."

Angela's heart skipped a beat. Something had happened.

"Is something wrong with Charlie?" she questioned, concern making her voice shake.

"No, not Charlie," Thomas quickly assured her. "Mr. Stratton has had a stroke."

"A stroke?" Angela thought of the man with his dour face

and his curt nods. She had always been a bit afraid of him. Now she pitied him. Perhaps if they had been kinder, more neighborly, the man might have softened a bit.

"Is it serious?" she asked, directing her question to Thane. He nodded slowly. "According to the report Pa got in the store, he's in pretty bad shape."

"So that's why we haven't seen much of Charlie for the last week or so," mused Thomas. "I was wondering why he hadn't been over to check on my spring plowing."

"Guess he's had his hands full just caring for his boss. Won't let anyone else do it, so I hear."

Charlie was withered and poorly himself. He shouldn't have to spend full time nursing another.

I must get over there, Angela said to herself, vowing she would go first thing the next morning.

Thane surprised her by changing the conversation abruptly. "I hear Trudie is throwing another party—she had so much fun at the last one."

Thane gave Thomas a teasing grin and punched him on the shoulder. Thomas reddened slightly but responded good-naturedly. "Jealous, old man?"

"Not on your life," continued Thane. "I have my eye on better things, but if you enjoy the chatter of a—" Thane stopped, suddenly realizing his remark would be in poor taste—"of a pretty little redhead," he finished lamely, "so be it."

For just a moment Angela felt a bit smug. Thane shared her opinion of Trudie. She stole a quick look at Thomas. Would he be offended? Hurt? But Thomas seemed totally unruffled by Thane's little slip. Angela sighed in relief and passed the cookies again.

"I'm planting a bit of that new seed," Thomas was saying. "The handful I tested is germinating well."

Thane turned to Thomas with a glow in his eyes. "Where is it?" he asked. "I'd like to see it."

Thomas ran for a lantern so he could lead Thane to the shed where he did his experimenting. Angela noticed excitement in both of them as they bounded down the steps, deep in conversation all the way to the small building.

———————

Early the next morning Angela wrapped a cake, fresh from the oven, and started off for the Stratton farm. It was a short distance across the stubble field and soon she was knocking on the door of the big house. She had never visited the Stratton home, and she held her breath as she stood before it, remembering the scowling face of the owner. The door opened tentatively at first, and then Charlie poked his head out. When he saw Angela he swung the door fully open.

"Come in. Come in, girlie," he invited.

Angela stepped into the wide front hall. The heavy shades on the windows had not been raised, so it took a minute for Angela's eyes to adjust to the darkness. When she got used to the veiled light she began to make out the objects lining the walls.

The place was much more formal and feminine looking than she would have guessed, having been inhabited by men for so many years. Angela knew Charlie was allowed the privilege of a downstairs bedroom, and Gus, the cook, lived somewhere else inside the big house. Mr. Stratton, according to town gossip, occupied the upper portion. Angela let her gaze lift gently up the long, ornate staircase. She wasn't sure who did the housekeeping chores. Rumor had it that Mr. Stratton would not allow a woman within the walls.

Charlie spoke from beside her, and Angela broke off her daydreaming.

"He's quite poorly," Charlie was saying as he accepted the cake Angela held out to him. "I don't s'pose yer anxious to be seein' him—him being like he is."

"No. No-o," faltered Angela. "I really came to see you, I guess. How—how are you managing?"

Charlie shook his head, sadness in his eyes. "Never thought I'd live to see the day when that big man had to take to his bed," he said simply.

"How are you managing?" Angela asked again.

"Me and Gus take turns. He needs someone night and day."

"Should you—should you get some outside help? Maybe Mrs.—"

"Boss wouldn't like thet much. He's not used to women fussin' around here."

"But if you need—"

"We'll manage jest fine," Charlie insisted. Then he turned their attention to other things. "C'mon to the kitchen. I'll fix us a cup of coffee."

Angela followed. She had never been in a man's kitchen before and she wasn't sure how Gus would keep his. When she saw him in town she had noticed that he was none too fussy about his own appearance. She expected his kitchen to reflect the same casual approach to things, but to her surprise the large, sunny room was in good order.

"My!" she exclaimed before she could check herself, "it is nice and clean in here."

Charlie grinned and then said soberly, "Gus'd have the head of anyone who messed up his kitchen. He's as fussy as an old woman 'bout it."

He cast a glance at Angela to see if she would take offense at his expression, but Angela paid no heed. She was much too busy gazing around the big room with its spacious cupboards and gleaming stove.

"It's nice," Angela murmured, more to herself than to Charlie. He nodded in acknowledgment and poured a handful of coffee into the pot. After adding some water, he placed the pot on the stove and put a few more sticks of wood on the fire.

"Sit down," he invited. "Sit down and tell me how things have been goin' at yer house. Since this here happened, I ain't been nowhere—or heard nothin'."

"Well, I guess nothing much has happened over our way," began Angela as she removed her bonnet and seated herself in a kitchen chair.

"Thomas started in the field yet?"

"Oh yes. He has most of the plowing finished."

"He gonna try some of thet there new seed?"

"A little. He doesn't dare plant much in case something

happens. He doesn't want to lose all his work. He did tell Thane the seed seems to be germinating fine, though."

Charlie shook his head and a bit of a grin pulled at the corners of his mouth. Angela knew he had a fatherly interest in them and was pleased with Thomas's success.

"If he gets him a good, sturdy seed for these parts, he will have done us all a great favor," Charlie commented.

As soon as the coffee boiled, Charlie poured a cup, cut a generous piece of the cake Angela had brought, and started for the door.

"I'll be back in jest a jiffy," he said over his shoulder. "I'll take this on up to Gus and see how things are goin'."

Angela nodded and sat stiffly in her chair as she listened to his lumbering footsteps climb the long stairs. A door opened and she heard voices, but they were too far away for her to make any sense of the words.

Soon Charlie was back, his expression sober. "Gus says there's been no change. We keep hopin', but it don't look good. Doc says he—he ain't likely to come out of it."

Angela didn't know whom she felt sorriest for. The crotchety rancher or his devoted foreman and cook. She knew both Charlie and Gus were suffering over the illness of their long-time boss.

"Is there anything we can do?" she asked Charlie. "I could take a shift with the nursing if—"

"No, no. You got 'nough to do carin' for those young'uns. Me an' Gus'll make out just fine."

"But what about the other work? The cattle and—"

"Got enough hired help around here thet they oughta be able to see to thet. About time thet some of them started to earn their keep," said Charlie with a wave of his hand.

They had their coffee together and Angela excused herself.

"Be sure to let us know if we can do anything," she said as she left. "You know we'd be glad to help out." She could have added, "After all you've done for us over the years," but she didn't. Charlie probably understood.

"I will. I will," promised Charlie. "Thet cake was mighty

appreciated. Gus hasn't been doin' his usual meal fixin' lately."

Angela left with the resolve that she would send over more baking in a couple of days and as often as she felt it was needed until things improved at the Stratton household. It was the least she could do to try to lighten their load.

————

"Come quick! Come quick!" Sara burst frantically into the room and grabbed Angela.

"What's wrong?" demanded Angela, grasping the young girl's shoulders and holding her at arms' length to look into her face.

"Louise!—" shrieked Sara.

"What happened?" Angela cried, shaking the slight shoulders. "Where is she? What happened?"

"She doesn't know."

"Where is she?" Angela repeated with another shake.

"In the bedroom," Sara managed to reply.

Angela released Sara and rushed to the bedroom, her heart hammering within her breast. Louise was there, lying across her bed, sobs shaking her body. *At least she is in one piece,* thought Angela with relief.

"What is it?" Angela asked, dropping to her knees beside the bed and lifting Louise into her arms.

"I—I think I'm—I'm dying," the child sobbed, a fresh torrent of tears running down her cheeks.

"What is it? Why? Are you ill? Did you—?"

"I don't know. I must be," sobbed the frightened girl.

Sara joined Louise in crying.

"Listen, both of you. Stop it. Stop the crying. Tell me what's wrong."

After asking only a few questions, Angela realized that her sister was not dying. Angela lifted herself from her knees to the bed and gathered Louise into her arms.

"You poor thing. You poor thing," she crooned, brushing her hair back from the flushed face.

"It's all right. You're fine. Really. You are just growing up, that's all. I should have known—should have thought—but I didn't. Mama would have known. She would have talked to you and prepared you. I'm sorry. I'm really sorry."

Angela looked from one girl to the other. They had both managed to quit crying. Their faces were still flushed and tear-streaked, and their shoulders still shook with an occasional sob, but they both seemed to be under control again.

Angela patted the bed beside her. "Climb up here beside us, Sara," she invited. "You are a bit young, but there is no help for it now. You might as well hear what I have to say to Louise."

Angela took a deep breath, trying hard to remember what her mother had said in their little chat years ago. She wasn't sure if she did it well, or if she was thoroughly understood by her two young sisters, but she did the best she could. In the end the faces were at peace again. Louise even managed a wobbly smile. Angela was only too glad to finish her mission and escape back to her kitchen.

Chapter Eight

The Unexpected

Thomas had worked hard in the field all day and was still warm and tired when he joined Angela on the veranda where she worked on the hem of a new dress for Louise.

"She's growing awfully fast, isn't she?" he observed, and Angela nodded. *Far too quickly as far as I'm concerned,* she thought.

"Do you think—" Thomas began, but Thane's arrival interrupted the thought.

"What are you up to?" Thomas called to Thane. "Can't your pa think of anything worthwhile to put you to doing?" he teased.

Thane stepped down from his horse and flipped the reins around the hitching post.

"Boy," said Thane, "I'm most ready to drop in my tracks, my pa's been working me so hard. If it hadn't been that I was worried some about my friend Tom, I would have just fallen in my bed and stayed right there."

Angela had heard the friendly bantering many times. She listened now with a slight smile. Thane was good for Thomas. His good-natured teasing helped lift the weight from her brother's young shoulders for a short time.

Angela laid aside the dress she was working on and went to get some refreshments.

"How's the new seed doing?" she heard Thane asking Thomas.

"Great. Just great. If we had more light, I'd show you. Why do you always come out here in the dark?"

"I tell you," responded Thane. "If I didn't come in the dark, I wouldn't get here at all. Pa's been pushing me at the store. He's adding a whole new section on the side. A big storage area and—"

Angela passed out of earshot. She could hear only the murmur of voices and an occasional hearty laugh.

When she returned with the milk and donuts the young men were talking about baseball. Angela passed the refreshments and picked up the garment again. It was too dark now to see well enough to finish the hem. With a sigh she laid the dress down again and settled in her chair to listen to the conversation.

Thane was quick to bring her in. "I hear you've been helping out the Stratton household with baking."

Angela nodded.

"Gus was in town for some supplies and he's been bragging all over town about what a top-notch cook you are."

"Nothing fancy about what I've been sending," said Angela, embarrassed. "Guess if one is hungry enough, anything tastes good."

Thane grinned and winked at Thomas. "Think you and I have tried enough of her cooking over the years to know it isn't hunger that causes a man to come back for more," he said, and Angela knew she had just been paid a nice compliment.

"How is Mr. Stratton?" asked Angela.

"Nobody is saying," responded Thane. "Even Doc is evasive. I don't think things are going well." Suddenly his tone changed. "Have you heard the latest bit of news?" he asked.

Angela shook her head.

"Mr. Stratton has a son."

"A son? I didn't even know he had a wife."

"I guess he doesn't—anymore. But he did at one time. Some of the older neighbors knew her—though they had almost forgotten she ever existed."

Angela's eyes opened wide. "Did she live here?" she asked.

"For a short time, it seems."

"That's why the house is so nicely decorated!" Angela exclaimed, feeling that the mystery was now solved.

"He built it for her. Tried to have it just the way she wanted. But she didn't like the West. She was from some big city back east, and I guess this life just didn't agree with her. She went back home. Took their baby boy with her. Folks say that Mr. Stratton hasn't seen either one of them since. That was some years ago."

Angela's face clouded. "How sad," she murmured softly. "Really sad. No wonder the poor man looks so gloomy all the time."

"But that's not all," Thane continued. "Rumor has it that the son is heading out this way. Seems that Charlie felt honor-bound to let him know of Mr. Stratton's condition, and the fellow has decided to come see for himself."

Angela smiled. Perhaps there would be a happy ending after all. She was glad for Mr. Stratton. She did hope that he was well enough to know and enjoy his grown-up son.

"Gus didn't sound too excited about it," Thane continued. "I think he fears that the fellow is just interested in getting his hands on the Stratton money."

Angela was suddenly angry. Why should Gus go and spoil her dream? Why couldn't it be concern—if not love—that was bringing the junior Stratton to his father's bedside?

"Well," she said defiantly, "perhaps Gus should wait and see before he brands the man as a black-heart. He could at least give him a chance."

"You're right," Thane responded, more serious now. "Maybe we all should."

"When is he to arrive?" asked Angela.

"I don't know. Soon, I gather from what Gus said. He was spreading the word around town, though he was none too happy about the situation."

"That's awful," Angela said, still annoyed. "The poor man hasn't even done anything, and already folks are against him. Fine welcome for someone coming to see his sick pa."

Angela resolved that she would not be one to brand a man

before she knew his intent. She promised herself she would take over some more baking the minute she learned of his arrival.

They spent the remainder of their evening talking of other things. After the moon had climbed high into the sky, Thane announced he'd better get on home.

Before leaving he reached into his shirt pocket and withdrew a small brown bag that he handed without comment to Angela. Like a small child, she could not resist a peek. Pink peppermints. Her favorite. She gave Thane a warm smile in thank you. He acknowledged it with a smile of his own, touched his cap, and was gone.

Mrs. Blackwell called. Even though she maintained that the young Petersons should be left strictly on their own, she still made it her neighborly duty to drop by now and then to see that they were doing things right. Angela had seen her coming and longed to slip out the back door and escape to the fields where Thomas and Derek were stacking the summer hay.

Instead, she laid aside her soiled apron and pushed the kettle forward on the stove to make a cup of tea.

Mrs. Blackwell was puffing her way up the veranda steps when Angela opened the door and smiled a welcome.

"My, that sun is hot today" was the only greeting the woman offered. She whisked off her heavy black bonnet and wiped her perspiring face.

Angela stepped aside to let her enter the kitchen. She headed directly for a chair beside the table, her eyes traveling hither and yon to survey the room.

"It's cool in here," she observed. "Guess you haven't been doin' any bakin' for a while."

"No," acknowledged Angela slowly, "when the weather is like this I try to do enough in one day to last us the week."

Mrs. Blackwell nodded her head but made no immediate comment. She wiped her face again and sat down heavily on the chair.

"How do you keep it fresh?" she asked forthrightly.

"We have an extra icebox in the shed out back. I wrap it and put it in there."

The woman frowned. Angela knew Mrs. Blackwell had no spare icebox and was probably thinking it wasn't fair that someone so young should have things she didn't.

"S'pose you heard about poor Mr. Stratton?" Mrs. Blackwell asked.

Angela nodded and willed the kettle to boil quickly.

"Such a shame. But then—jest another reminder thet the Lord don't take kindly to sin. One reaps what one sows—jest as the Book says."

Angela was glad she could turn to lift the teapot down from the shelf and not have to comment.

"You use that one for everyday? My, looks to me like your mama would have kept thet for special occasions."

"Mama felt it a special occasion when a neighbor came to call," Angela answered sweetly and gave the woman a nice smile.

Mrs. Blackwell flushed an even deeper red and busied herself with fanning for several moments before she found her tongue again.

"This here Mr. Stratton—has him a son. Did ya ever hear of such a thing? Comin' on out. Seems to me it woulda set better had he been here all those years helpin' his pa out. Might have saved his heart, or whatever the man has, iffen he would've been here. Doc won't say none what's ailin' the fella."

Angela set two china cups and saucers on the table and went for the cream and sugar.

"Well, I'm thinkin' thet he'll likely scoop up what he can get his hands on an' head straight back east to his mama— thet's what I'm thinkin'. He's probably a chip off the old block—as stingy and unneighborly as his pa. I remember the woman—shouldn't you let that tea steep a bit longer?—she was a flighty thing, let me tell you. Pretty as a picture—an' 'bout as flimsy. Couldn't lift her hand in her own kitchen. An' the mister. He tried to give her everything so thet she would be happy here. We knew it would never work. Some of us tried to tell him, but he jest turned a deaf ear. Well, I guess he learned."

Angela set the tea before Mrs. Blackwell and turned for the sponge cake.

"Yer brothers hayin'?" the woman asked.

Angela nodded.

"Wonder iffen it's quite dry enough. You can sure ruin good hay iffen you don't give it time to dry proper."

Angela bit her lip and then boldly suggested that they thank the Lord for the refreshments. Mrs. Blackwell looked surprised, as though tea and cake were hardly worth a prayer.

Angela's prayer was simple and sincere. When she lifted her head she passed the cake to her neighbor.

"Those sisters of yours big enough to be of any use to you yet?" asked Mrs. Blackwell as she stirred the cream and sugar into her tea.

"They have always been of use to us," responded Angela a bit too quickly.

"Work? Work?" hurried on Mrs. Blackwell in explanation. "Are they able to help with—?"

"Oh yes," cut in Angela. "They've had their own chores from when they were tiny—which they see to on their own," she informed the older woman, feeling a bit smug.

"Where are they now?" asked Mrs. Blackwell, her eyes traveling about as though she thought the two young girls should be scurrying about the kitchen.

"I sent them out to pick strawberries for jam," replied Angela.

"It's a bit late for strawberries."

"Oh no. The girls brought in a nice pailful yesterday. I canned five jars of jam with it."

The woman seemed to be at a loss as to what to say next. She took a bite of her sponge cake and turned again to Angela.

"I'm guessin' you've been a bit wasteful in usin' eggs. I have a way of making this same recipe with about half the eggs. Eggs are worth money, you know. Every egg saved means—"

"We have lots of eggs," said Angela softly.

"Still—you can take 'em to town and sell 'em. Trade 'em fer something needed. No sense being wasteful—"

Louise burst through the door. In her hand was a pail filled with bright red strawberries. "We found the best patch—" she began but jerked to a halt when she saw the woman at the table. "Excuse me," she said softly. "Hello, Mrs. Blackwell."

Sara moved in beside her sister, her face flushed and streaks of dirt on her pinafore. But her blue eyes were dancing, and Angela knew she was nearly bursting with excitement over some find. But Sara held her tongue and curtsied slightly. "Hello, Mrs. Blackwell," she said in no more than a whisper.

Angela could have hugged them both. They had remembered their manners. She felt pride swelling within her. Her mama would have been so pleased.

"Wash your hands," she instructed, her voice shaky with emotion, "and you can have a slice of sponge cake and a glass of milk."

Mrs. Blackwell collected her thoughts and spoke again. "Won't thet spoil their supper?"

"They have worked hard," replied Angela firmly. "And growing children must be fed."

She sliced generous pieces of the cake and poured out two chilled glasses of milk as the girls washed at the corner basin.

"You may take it to the back porch out of the sun," she told Louise and Sara as she handed them the food.

Mrs. Blackwell may have felt that Angela did not trust two rowdy children at the same table as a neighborhood guest. But in truth, there was no way Angela would have subjected her two young sisters to the tiresome exchange she was enduring.

Chapter Nine

The Son

"Well, he's here," Thomas announced as he hoisted the box of groceries onto the kitchen table. "Thane said that Gus came into town almost bursting."

"Who's here?" asked Angela, reaching for the bag of sugar.

"The young Mr. Stratton. Don't even know his name. No one seems to know his name."

"Is he—is he like his father?" asked Angela hesitantly.

Thomas laughed. "I haven't laid eyes on him myself, but from what folks are saying, he is pretty citified. Don't expect he'll last long out here."

"Thomas, don't be like the others and brand him bad before he even gets a chance to prove himself," Angela reprimanded gently.

Thomas moved to the corner stand and lifted a dipper of cold water. He drank long and deeply before he lowered the dipper. With a quick movement of his wrist, he splashed the remaining water into the blue basin and returned the dipper to the pail.

"You're right," he said seriously. "We need to give the fellow a chance."

He reached out and ruffled Angela's hair as he headed for the door. "I'm going to be working on that last hay field. Send Derek out as soon as he has his chores done."

Angela nodded and lifted the salt and baking soda from the grocery box. Already her mind was rushing. Should she

71

bake a chocolate cake or a batch of fudge brownies to take to the Strattons? She still felt it was a shame how folks were so willing to think ill of the young Mr. Stratton even before they knew him.

It was fudge brownies that Angela delivered to the Stratton household later in the day. She was not as timid when she stepped up to rap on the door as she had been when she had made her first delivery to the big house. Over the weeks the little trip across the field to see Charlie—or Gus—had become a welcomed break in her routine day.

She looked about her now before lifting her hand to the wooden door. Flowers were blooming in the bed to the right. She wondered who had the time or interest to plant flowers, and then quickly attributed them to Charlie. Charlie, though elderly and crippled, liked pretty things.

Angela knocked and waited, expecting Charlie to pop his head out the door. But the door was opened by a stranger. Angela blinked, then stepped quickly back and felt her face flushing.

She had never before seen anyone dressed quite like he was. His long tailored suit jacket with velvet lapels hung open over a matching vest. A gold chain stretched across his front from button hole to side pocket. A carefully knotted scarf at the throat of his stark-white stand-up collar added a softening touch to the otherwise stiff-looking attire. Softly striped trousers and highly polished boots were the last things Angela noticed before remembering her manners. Her eyes moved quickly back to the man's face.

His complexion was pale and looked baby-soft, as though neither sun nor rain had ever touched it. And his hair seemed as though wind never tousled it. Every shining strand was carefully combed into place. Slight waves hinted at curliness, but Angela somehow was sure they were never allowed to get out of control.

He seemed so foreign to Angela that she felt confused. He did not belong to the world she was used to. She hardly knew how to address him. Her flush deepened.

"H—Hello," she finally stammered. "I—I am looking for Mr. Stratton."

The gentleman tipped his head slightly while she awkwardly tried to tuck in a strand of silvery blond hair that danced playfully about her face in the afternoon breeze. Her blue eyes, wide in astonishment, and her flushed cheeks revealed her confusion.

Then he offered a smile—not a friendly grin like Angela was used to receiving from Charlie but a smile—soft, curving, and controlled.

"I do hope you are a neighbor," he said in a deep, resonant voice. "A close neighbor."

"I—I'm Angela," she murmured and felt even more foolish. "I—I—expected Charlie—"

"Charlie is busy."

"Oh—of course. Well, really I came to see Mr. Stratton and well—"

"I'm sorry," he said, kind but firm. "He really isn't up to visitors. He's quite ill."

"Oh, not that Mr. Stratton," Angela said quickly. "I mean the—the new Mr. Stratton." She knew she had said it all wrong. She tried again. "Mr. Stratton's son."

The door swung open to its full width and the youthful gentleman stepped back and bid her enter with a wave of his hand. The smile had returned.

"That Mr. Stratton would be most pleased to see you." He motioned Angela into the hallway. "Won't you come into the parlor?"

Angela stumbled along in step.

"Please be seated," he continued. "I will have Gus prepare some coffee—or perhaps you prefer tea?"

Angela had never been in the parlor before. Her wide eyes studied it now, going from the gold damask of the sofa and chairs to the rich mahogany of the piano. She wanted to just stand and look, but the man beside her seemed to be asking her something. She turned her attention back to him and shook her head slightly.

"I—I'm sorry," she murmured.

"Tea—or coffee?" he repeated.

"I—I think—tea, please," she managed to answer and then remembered the pan in her hands. "I—I've brought some baking," she said. "To sort of welcome the—the other Mr. Stratton—to the community—as a neighbor—you know." She thrust the pan out toward the stranger.

She had never been so flustered before. Was this young man Mr. Stratton's lawyer? Maybe he had accompanied the son here. If only he would stop looking at her. If only Charlie would make an appearance.

"Please," the young man said again. "Won't you have a chair. I'll only be a minute." As soon as Angela had taken the seat he offered, he left, baking in hand.

Angela arranged her skirts carefully and wiped her palms on her pocket handkerchief. Before she could turn her attention back to the identity of the stranger and to her intriguing surroundings, she heard footsteps in the hall and turned to see Charlie enter the room. She could have hugged him. He crossed to her and took her trembling hand.

"Are you ill, girlie?" he asked, noticing her flushed face and clammy fingers.

"Oh, Charlie," she admitted, "I have just made such a fool of myself. I—I came over here to—to sort of welcome Mr. Stratton's son with some baking and I—I expected you—or Gus—to open the door and it—it quite threw me when this—this total stranger was standing there, and I've been babbling like a silly schoolgirl ever since."

Charlie gave Angela a quizzical look. Then his hand tightened. "He threw ya, did he?" he asked, and Angela detected annoyance in his voice.

"Oh, it wasn't that. I mean he was most polite," she hurried on. "It was just that I expected you—or Gus—or maybe even Mr. Stratton's son, but—"

"Angela," said Charlie giving her hand a bit of a shake, "that *was* Mr. Stratton's son."

Angela looked at Charlie with wide eyes, unable to believe that he was serious. She wasn't sure what she had expected—

perhaps just a younger version of the older perhaps, with a gloomy, weathered face, dusty boots, and a buckskin jacket.

"That—?"

Charlie nodded.

"But—but—he is so *young!*"

Charlie nodded again.

"He—he's not much older than—than Thomas!" exclaimed Angela.

"A little," said Charlie.

"But I thought—I mean, I expected—well—someone quite—quite different."

"I apologize that I took so long," said a cultured voice from the doorway. "I couldn't find Gus so I had to make the tea myself. I do hope—" Then the young man spotted Charlie. "Oh, Charlie—" he said and let the words hang.

"Gus is with your father," Charlie explained, then turned back to Angela. "I'll try to get over one of these evenings," he said, giving her hand a final squeeze. Angela nodded and watched him leave the room.

"Cream and sugar?" asked her young host after a few moments of awkward silence.

"No—no thank you. Neither," Angela managed to reply, and then she took charge of herself. *I need not be flustered,* she informed herself. *My mama taught me to be a lady, so I will act like one.* Angela willed her racing heart and trembling hands to be quiet. Soon she sat at tea in the big parlor as though she had done so for many years.

"I must offer my apology," she said shyly. "I did not realize that Mr. Stratton's son would be so young; therefore I did not realize who you were when you opened the door."

He answered with a playful smile, as proper and controlled as his laugh had been.

"I do hope you have not been disappointed," he said.

Angela was quite shocked when she realized she had fluttered her eyelashes in response.

"Now—you must tell me about yourself," he invited engagingly. "You are Angela. Do you have a last name, Angela?"

She laughed a light, silvery laugh and looked fully at the

young man before her. "My, I did appear like a simpleton, didn't I?" she admitted, and then hurried on. "My name is Angela Peterson."

"And you live—?"

Angela was beginning to relax and decided to allow herself to enjoy the afternoon tea.

"I could say, just over the stubble field," she replied, "but I guess it would be more proper to say, on the farm adjoining your land to the left. Well, one of the farms on the left. I realize that your land stretches far enough to border several farms on each side."

He accepted the acknowledgment of the Stratton wealth with a slight smile and a nod of his head.

"And you are the Angel of Mercy who has been bearing sustenance to Charlie and Gus since the illness of my father."

It was his compliment to her, but for just a moment her breath caught in her throat. A distant memory had been awakened of a little girl with silvery pigtails flying in the wind, running toward the outstretched arms of a man with hair of the same color. He was a tall man, with broad shoulders and strong arms, and as he swept up the girl and enfolded her against his chest, she heard her father's words, "And how is my Angel?"

Yes, she thought, *Father used to call me that. I had forgotten.* Angela fought to return to the present so she might give the proper response to the young man before her.

———

The Petersons played the memory game again. Angela could hardly wait for her turn so she could tell them her memory of her father's pet name for her.

As usual Sara was given the first turn. "I 'member—remember—I remember," she said, her brow puckered in deep concentration; then her eyes brightened. "I remember when Papa took me to the circus and bought me lots of treats and showed me big elephants and walking bears and—"

"Sara," cut in Louise. "You never went to the circus."

"I did, too," argued Sara, her lower lip beginning to protrude.

"You did not," insisted Louise before anyone else could comment. "There was never a circus here to go to."

"Louise is right," said Angela slowly. "You must have had a dream."

Louise wasn't as gracious to her young sister as Angela had been. "That's a lie," she condemned Sara. "We aren't ever to tell lies."

Sara's pouting lip began to tremble; then a flood of tears followed. "Well, I can't 'member anymore," she sobbed. "Everyone has more to talk about than me."

Angela took the small girl into her arms and soothed her. "Sh-h-h," she whispered. "It's okay. That's why we are playing the game, remember? So those of us who have more memories can share them with you. Sh-h-h."

At last Sara was quieted and Angela knew that it was her turn to make a statement.

"But Louise is right. You must never tell stories as—as truths if they are not. Papa and Mama would never tolerate tales of any kind. You must remember that in the future."

With that understanding, the game went on.

"I remember," said Louise, "when Papa brought a whole big box of apples home from town and he let me have one to eat—even before Mama made pie or sauce or anything. It was—yummy."

Even Sara laughed as Louise rolled her eyes and rubbed her tummy.

It was Derek's turn. His contributions had been a bit more open recently, his comments a bit lengthier. But both Thomas and Angela knew he was still a troubled boy.

"I remember—" began Derek, and then a frown creased his brow. He swallowed hard, seeming determined to go on. "I remember—the—the day Mama died."

Angela caught her breath. Thomas moved as though to reach out a hand to his young brother, then quickly withdrew it. "Yes?" he prompted.

"I remember—I brought her a bird shell—just a little blue

one—it was in two pieces—the baby had already hatched—
but I knew she would like to see it."

He stopped and swallowed again. His eyes did not lift from
his empty dinner plate.

"I—I tiptoed into her bedroom—I thought she might be
asleep—then I—I touched her hand."

There was a pause again and Angela feared that Derek
might not be able to go on.

"It was cold," he managed after some time. "I—I whispered
to her—but she didn't open her eyes. Then I—I shook her—
just a little bit."

The room was chilled and quiet. Not a person moved. Not
an eye lifted from their brother's pale face.

"Then I—I shook her harder—and she still didn't wake up.
I started to get scared. I shook her again. Then I started to
cry, and then—then Mrs. Barrows opened the door and looked
at me, and she frowned at me and said, 'Your Mama is gone,
boy. Mustn't cry, now. You're a big boy,' and I ran past her and
I ran and ran until I was out of breath and—"

Tears were now falling freely down Derek's cheeks.
Thomas reached for him, pulled him close, and held him. Angela, through tears of her own, quietly led the two young girls,
also weeping, out of the kitchen. As she left she could hear
Thomas's gentle voice. "That's right. Go ahead and cry. Just
cry it all out. I never heard Papa say that a man couldn't cry
when he had good reason."

From the tremor in Thomas's voice, Angela knew he was
shedding tears of his own.

"Oh, God," she prayed, "help poor little Derek. Wash his
memory of this—this terrible hurt—and touch his soul with
your healing. Might he be—be freed from the past now—and
be able to go on."

Chapter Ten

A Birthday

"Why don't you go? I really don't have much time for a party," Angela said to Thomas.

It's you who Trudie wants anyway, she was thinking, but she didn't voice it.

Thomas was shaking his head. "Nope. You don't go, I don't go."

Angela was a bit annoyed and a little surprised at his response. He usually was not so stubborn.

"Truth is, I didn't really have much fun at the last one. And I hate to leave the—"

"They were fine last time—remember?"

Angela had to admit that the children had gotten along perfectly well without them for a few hours.

"I really don't see why—"

Thomas cut her short. "You need to get out. You didn't have fun last time because you had forgotten how. You are not a little old lady, Angela. You are seventeen."

"Eighteen," corrected Angela with a deep sigh.

"All right, eighteen," Thomas agreed. "Tomorrow you'll be eighteen. But that's still a long way from eighty, and that's how you're acting. Now get yourself all prettied up and let's get over there—before the party is over and the food is all gone," teased Thomas.

Reluctantly Angela pulled herself from her chair and put aside the sock she had been darning. She didn't feel one bit like partying. Especially not at Trudie's house.

It did not take her long to change her dress and pin her hair firmly into place. She dusted a bit of fine flour across her nose and tucked a clean hankie into her pocket. She knew she wouldn't enjoy this evening, but Thomas seemed to have his heart set on going, and Angela did not want to spoil it for him. After all, Thomas was not old either, and he had certainly missed out on his share of fun.

It could get cool later in the evening, so Angela grabbed a shawl and went to meet Thomas at the kitchen door. She was expecting a bit of a fuss from Louise, who felt she was old enough to be in on the entertainment of the young folks of the community. And Louise didn't care much for her appointed task of the evening.

Angela had posted all three youngsters at the kitchen table to do review lessons. She believed it was important over the summer months to have them study what they had learned the year before. They often argued vociferously, saying that none of the other mothers demanded so much from their offspring, but Angela held firm, and one evening a week was deemed "study night."

Angela was about to release them from tonight's assignment and tell them they could read a book of their choice instead. It didn't seem fair that they had to study while she partied. But when she entered the kitchen all three were working diligently. Louise hardly lifted her head.

"We won't be long," Angela promised, and Derek raised his eyes for a moment and nodded. Louise and Sara kept their eyes on the opened books before them. Angela shrugged. It seemed that Thomas was the only one with any enthusiasm for the party.

Thomas helped her climb into the wagon, and then they were off.

It was a clear evening and the moon was just coming up. Angela decided to forget her ill humor and enjoy the ride. The fields of ripening grain stretched along beside the roadway, promising another good harvest.

Dear God, don't let anything happen to it, Angela prayed

silently. *We need it so. The children need new things for school. They grow so fast, I can hardly keep up with them. And Thomas—it's been years since he's had a new suit, and I have let down every hem and let out every seam and he still looks like a little boy on a growing spurt instead of like a man. And I know it must embarrass him some, Lord, even if he doesn't say.*

Angela stole a look at Thomas. He had filled out to be almost the size her father had been. In fact, he reminded her more of their papa every day in appearance and carriage.

Thomas must have felt her eyes on him, for he turned and gave her a grin. "Still mad?" he teased.

Angela dipped her head. How could she be angry with Thomas? He deserved to have a good time. If he wished to party—then she would party. Though she still couldn't understand why he had insisted that she go along.

She gave Thomas a reluctant smile. "No. I'm not mad," she responded, and the smile came in its fullness.

"Good!" was all he answered, and he turned his attention back to the horses.

They rode in silence for several moments, then Angela turned to her brother and asked a blunt question. "Thomas, if you could be anything you wanted—do anything you wanted—would you be a farmer?"

Thomas looked directly at her and his eyes seemed to darken slightly. He appeared reluctant to answer, but he finally began to shake his head slowly.

"Don't you like to farm?"

"Well—it's not—not that I don't like it—really. It's just that I think there is something I would like better."

"I never knew that," Angela replied softly. "But then, I never even thought about it before."

There was silence again. Finally Angela took up the conversation again.

"What is it that you think you'd like better?" she asked.

"Research," he said without hesitation. "With grains and fruits and things."

Angela nodded. She should have known. Thomas was always working with his seeds and hybrids.

"But you do that now," she reminded him.

"Not the way I'd like to. I have no space—no training—no proper equipment. And very little time," he finished with a sigh.

Angela nodded her head. He was right. He did have very little time and he did not have the proper tools or the room to work. More than once his precious plants had frozen and he had been set back in his experimentation. Angela hadn't realized until now what a great disappointment that must have been for him.

They rode in silence again while Angela mulled over the dream Thomas had just shared. *If it wasn't for the children,* she was thinking, *Thomas might have a chance to work with his seeds. I could find a job or—*But there was no use dreaming. The children needed his care.

"And you?" asked Thomas.

Angela came back from her reverie with a start and looked at her older brother. She shrugged and shifted her shawl in her lap.

"Oh, I don't know. Nothing I guess. At least nothing like that. There was a time when I thought I would like to be a teacher, but not anymore. I would have liked to go to school more, though. Just to learn. I had to quit so early. But then, I guess one never needs to stop learning—from books and—and everything in life. I can read the lesson books the children bring home."

"Is that why you are so—so—"

Angela knew Thomas thought she was too hard on the kids about their studies. He had never fully agreed with her regarding the summer review sessions, but he had always backed her.

"Is that why you are so determined that the three of them make the most of their studies?" he finished at last.

Angela nodded. "It seems such a shame not to get all they can out of their years in school. They are over all too soon anyway—and then adult responsibilities crowd in and take over and there is no more time to learn from books," Angela said soberly.

Thomas nodded.

"Yet," said Angela hesitantly, "I almost let them off tonight. It just didn't seem fair that we were off to a party and they had to sit there at the kitchen table with their lesson books. But they were so intent when we left that I decided not to disturb them." Then Angela changed the subject. "Who's going to be at the party?" she asked.

"The usual, I guess," answered Thomas. Angela wondered why his casual answer didn't match his rather knowing expression.

"Who's going to be there?" she repeated.

"I guess we'll see when we get there" was all Thomas would say as he clucked to the horse.

When they entered the Sommerses' yard and Angela saw the number of teams tied to the fence posts, she thought the whole community must be there.

"Looks like Trudie is throwing quite a party," she murmured.

Thomas tied the team and extended his arm to Angela. She took it and let him escort her around to the back of the house. There didn't seem to be anyone around and Angela was about to suggest that they try the front door instead.

As they rounded the corner an explosion of sound greeted them. "Surprise." "Surprise." "Happy birthday." "Happy Birthday." The shouts were coming at Angela from all sides as heads began to pop out from behind every tree and shrub.

Angela drew a quick breath, and Thomas had to hold fast to the hand tucked in his arm.

It was then that Angela noticed the streamers strung in the tree branches. And then an even more amazing sight caught her attention. There were Derek, Louise, and Sara, dressed in their Sunday finery and yelling right along with the rest of the crowd, "Surprise! Surprise!"

"How did you get here?" Angela stammered.

"We cut across the field," Louise called cheerily, and Angela knew she had the answer to their diligent studying. Louise was getting in on the party after all.

The evening was a blur to Angela. She had never been the

guest of honor at a party before—and she wasn't sure how much she enjoyed being the center of attention now. Still, she did appreciate all the effort Trudie had put into the event. She determined to be kinder, a little more tolerant of her friend— until she spotted Trudie hovering around Thomas again. *My— what a good deal of time and expense just to get Thomas over here,* Angela mused. Thomas had turned down each invitation to the other parties Trudie proposed, up till now. Angela shook her head. Some girls were so foolish.

Angela noticed that Thomas did not devote his total evening to Trudie. He mixed easily through the crowd, chatting and laughing and teasing. He truly seemed to be enjoying himself.

Derek hung back some, but gradually joined the younger boys. They mostly sat and watched the older ones. Angela decided that perhaps they were studying the older youths so they would know how to behave when it was their turn.

Louise was more socially inclined and made repeated attempts to join in. Angela knew how much her sister longed to be a part of everything that was going on while still feeling unsure of herself. Angela ached for the young girl. "It just takes time," she whispered under her breath. "Don't try to rush it, Louise. You'll be an adult soon enough."

Sara, still a little girl in the eyes of most of the partygoers, was pampered and fussed over. Sara enjoyed the spotlight and seemed to feel that she deserved every nod and smile. She bounced about, chattering and giggling and accepting every goodie offered to her.

They played party games and a few jokes on one another. Then Angela had to cut the enormous birthday cake and serve the pieces to each one present. By the time she had finished giving out the cake, the others had finished eating and were busy chatting and teasing again. Trudie suggested a sing-song, looking at Thomas for his answer.

"Not tonight," he answered. "When I get singing I hate to stop and I have to get the younger ones home."

Louise gave Thomas an impatient scowl.

"Angela can stay," Thomas was quick to say. "I'll leave the

team for her and we'll walk across the field."

"I'll drive her home," offered Thane.

"But I—I should—" began Angela.

"Nonsense," Thomas replied. "It's your birthday party. You stay and sing. I'll tuck them in."

Louise pushed out her lip, but a word from her older brother quickly erased the pout. Angela wondered what Thomas had whispered to her.

Trudie looked about as upset as Louise. For a moment she stood silently, her face clouded with disappointment. Then she flipped her reddish hair and crossed to Thomas. She laid a hand on his sleeve and looked up at him with her long eyelashes fluttering slightly. "You can come back after you've tucked them in," Angela heard her say.

"We'll see," nodded Thomas as Angela turned away.

Thomas gathered up the three younger ones and they headed for home, calling their thank yous over and over as they left. They had enjoyed the party; and Angela was glad, for their sakes, that she had consented to come.

The singing began and Angela found herself tucked between the preacher's two sons. They sang heartily, one a bass, the other a tenor, of sorts—he never could quite find the right notes.

Angela found it easy to forgive the missed notes, but the constant shuffling and vying for her attention unnerved her.

"I just turned nineteen," Roger informed her.

Angela congratulated him.

"I'm only six months younger," said Peter from the other side, edging a bit closer and making Angela feel uncomfortable.

They began another song and Angela joined in heartily, glad for a chance to put an end to the conversation.

At the first break, Peter whispered in her ear, "You want anything? Cake or more punch or anything?"

Angela graciously declined.

"Your shawl?" asked Roger, pointing to where Angela's shawl still hung on a nearby shrub.

Angela wondered how he could possibly think she needed

her shawl. She felt so crowded that she was overly warm, not cool.

"No thank you. I'm fine," she responded.

"It's a nice evening, isn't it?" said Roger. "I bet the stars would really show up away from the campfire. Would you like to walk around a bit?"

Angela declined that offer as well.

She turned her head slightly to see Thane standing just to their left. It was not hard to catch his eye.

She mouthed the words "I think I'm ready to go," and he must have been able to read her lips. He came immediately to where she was sitting, offered her his hand, and helped her up from her sitting position on the grass.

Angela smiled her good night to two disappointed young men and wound her way through the crowd of young people to thank her hostess.

"When you get home you can tell Thomas—" Trudie began.

Angela nodded in understanding, thanked her for the party and turned to go before Trudie could return to her sentence.

It was a beautiful evening. Even now Angela did not need her shawl. She tossed it carelessly over the back of Thane's buggy seat and sighed deeply as she looked up at the multitude of stars. The moon cast a soft mystic light on the world about her.

"Have fun?" asked Thane.

"I—I guess I did," answered Angela. She would never have thought to be anything but candid with Thane. Besides, he knew her so well that he would not have been fooled anyway. "I certainly got the surprise of my life. Why, I never dreamed that—that anyone would have remembered my birthday."

They rode in silence for a few moments and then Angela asked abruptly, "Has Thomas ever talked to you about—about his—his longing to work with seeds—as a researcher?"

"He shows them to me all the time."

"No, I mean to really work with plants and things—in a big—Where do they work with seeds, anyway?"

"In a laboratory, I guess—or out in small fields or something."

"Well, wherever. He would like to do that."

Thane nodded. He didn't seem at all surprised.

"What would you like to do?" asked Angela. "If you could do anything you wanted to."

"Marry a pretty girl," responded Thane without a moment's hesitation.

"Be serious," protested Angela, giving him a little push.

"Oh, I am," he insisted, but there was teasing in his voice.

"No, really. Tell me. If you could do anything you would like."

"Farm," said Thane, and Angela could not have been more surprised at his answer.

"Farm?" she echoed.

She looked at him, her eyes big in the moonlight. "Are you really serious?" she asked.

"Why do you think I spend so much time out at your place?" he asked, and Angela could hear the teasing again.

"You're joshing," she said.

His voice softened. "You want the truth. The real truth. Okay. I really would farm. I have always loved helping Tom and learning about planting and harvesting and caring for the animals. But that is not the reason I spend as much time as I can at your place."

Angela knew he was serious now.

"Are you surprised?"

"Yes," said Angela. "Yes, I guess I am. Does your—your pa know?"

"About my wanting to farm—or my reason for visiting your place?" Thane was quiet for a minute and then went on. "It doesn't seem too likely that I ever will farm, so I haven't really said anything to anyone."

Angela nodded slowly and then reached out and took Thane's arm. Thane gave her hand a slight squeeze in response.

"It's really strange, isn't it?" Angela said. "Thomas is farming and he wants to leave and do something else. You work with your father in a good business in town—and you want to farm. It seems that life gets terribly mixed up at times." Angela sighed deeply.

"And you?" asked Thane.

"I—I want you both to be happy," replied Angela with deep feeling.

"But for you?" prompted Thane. "What do you want to do?"

"Oh, I don't know," sighed Angela, but tears formed in the corners of her eyes. "For now—I guess—I guess I just want to care for the youngsters—to try to raise them as Mama would have. And I can't. It's too big a job for me, Thane."

"You are doing just fine," Thane assured her, pressing her hand lightly.

Angela pulled out her handkerchief and dabbed her eyes. Then her chin lifted slightly. She looked ready to take up her task.

"And what about your life?" Thane pressed. "They won't need you forever. Don't you think you have the right to make some plans of your own?"

"I don't know," said Angela honestly. "I try not to think ahead any further than to getting the children raised."

They reached the farmyard and Thane stepped down from the buggy and turned to lend a hand to Angela. He led her to the veranda and up the steps. He still had not released her hand.

"Tired?" he asked.

Angela responded with a shrug of her shoulders.

"I guess I am. I—I'm not sure I'm ready for sleep, but I'd better go in. Thomas might want to go back for the sing-song."

"Is that why you left early?"

Angela laughed. A soft, good-humored laugh. "The real reason," she confided, "was because those Merrifield boys had me smothered."

"I noticed," said Thane, sounding a bit annoyed. "I'd a liked to have banged their heads together—"

"Well, it was time to leave anyway," Angela responded quickly. "Thanks for bringing me home. I'd better go in."

"I—I have something for you—before you go." Thane

reached into a pocket of his coat.

"What—?" began Angela.

"A little birthday gift."

"Oh-h-h, Thane!" exclaimed Angela, "You shouldn't—"

"Now don't try to tell me what I should or shouldn't do," he chuckled. "Turn around," he instructed softly, and Angela did as bidden.

He reached his arms over her shoulders to settle something around her neck. In the moonlight she saw it glisten, but it was too dark for her to make it out properly. Thane fastened it without a fumble and then Angela felt something pressed lightly against her hair. Her breath caught. It was as though—as though he had kissed the top of her head like her papa used to do with her mama. But no—surely Thane wouldn't.

"There," he said, his lips close to her ear. "Happy birthday. I do hope that we—that you—will have many, many more."

"Thank you," she whispered back, wondering why they were speaking so softly. "Thank you. I can—can hardly wait to get into the light so I can see—"

He laughed at her. A soft, merry laugh. "Well, off you go then. Sweet dreams."

She stepped away, then back again. Thane had not moved. "Thane," she said, her voice breathless, "thank you so much for—for everything." She reached up on tiptoe and gave him a light kiss on the cheek, then hurried across the veranda and into the house.

Thomas was sitting at the kitchen table reading one of the study books. He lifted his head when she entered the room and she pointed to the cameo that hung from her neck on its silver chain. She lifted it with trembling fingers and studied it closely in the light.

"From Thane," she said softly, her eyes sparkling. "For my birthday."

Thomas nodded, showing no surprise at her announcement.

"Isn't it just—just beautiful?" whispered Angela, and she moved toward the stairs with misty eyes. She forgot all about asking Thomas if he wished to go back to the party.

Chapter Eleven

Harvest

As the days moved toward harvest, Angela found herself extremely busy. Thomas suggested that Louise stay home from school for a few days to help, but Angela would hear none of it. Thomas did not argue.

Angela had very little time to think about neighbors, but one day she quizzed Thomas as he hurriedly ate his dinner in the field. "Have you heard how Mr. Stratton is doing?"

"Which Mr. Stratton?"

"You know the one I mean," she said impatiently.

"Haven't you been delivering your baked goods lately?"

"You know I haven't had time—and Charlie hasn't been over for—for just ages."

"Poor Charlie," Thomas commented, and Angela's eyes opened wide with concern.

"He's on duty night and day, I hear," Thomas went on to explain. "If he wasn't so attached to that crotchety old man, I'm sure he would have left by now."

"I don't know how he manages," agreed Angela. "Nursing Mr. Stratton and running the ranch—"

"Oh, he doesn't run the ranch anymore," Thomas interrupted.

Angela swung her head to look at him.

"The son took over as boss of the ranch," Thomas explained. "About as soon as he got here he made it clear that

91

he would be giving the orders. Charlie was told he was official nursemaid, nothing more."

"How awful!" exclaimed Angela. "Charlie has always been foreman at the ranch."

Angela gathered up the lunch things and started back to her kitchen, pondering the new information as she picked her way home through the stubble field.

If Charlie really had been assigned new duties, he must be feeling pretty bad about it, she reasoned. Charlie had loved the ranch and working with the cattle. Angela always got the impression that the herds were sort of like family, or friends, to old Charlie.

"I should get over there," Angela mused out loud. "Charlie might really be feeling down—and too busy to come calling."

In spite of her already busy day, Angela prepared a cake for the oven and determined to deliver it as soon as it cooled.

It didn't take her long to hurry across the fields separating the Petersons from the Strattons. Soon she was rapping lightly on the door of the big house. She recalled her last visit and her surprise when the young Mr. Stratton had answered her knock. She wondered if he would be the one at the door again today. She flushed slightly as she looked down at her Sunday dress. She had changed from her working frock—just in case. And she had pinned her hair a bit more carefully as well, and fastened on her most becoming bonnet.

But it was Gus who opened the door. He seemed genuinely pleased to see her and with great enthusiasm invited her inside.

Angela, recovering quickly from just a twinge of disappointment, said, "I'm sorry it's been so long. We've been so busy with the harvest and all."

"Of course. Of course," replied Gus, ushering her into the kitchen. "We haven't been expectin' you with everything you have to do. Sit down. Sit down. I'll jest put on some fresh coffee before I call Charlie."

"How is—?" Angela was going to say "Charlie," but she changed her mind, thinking that she would wait and see for herself. "How is Mr. Stratton?" she asked instead.

"He's poorly. Poorly," answered Gus, repeating himself, a little habit he had.

"I'm sorry," said Angela. "It must be awfully hard for all of you."

Gus nodded. "Tough. Tough," he admitted, his eyes clouding.

Gus did not have to leave the kitchen to call Charlie. Angela heard a step on the back stairs and Charlie entered the room looking tired and old. Angela had never seen him looking so down. He had not even shaved.

His eyes brightened when he saw her, and he straightened his bent shoulders just a bit.

"I've been worried about you," Angela admitted, and Charlie gave her a nod.

"I hear he is no better," Angela went on.

Charlie settled himself in a chair across from her at the small kitchen table and rubbed a hand over his unshaven face. A look of shock filled his eyes, as though he suddenly realized how he must look to the young girl.

"Didn't have time—" he began apologetically, but Angela would not let him finish.

"I hear you are nursing night and day. You must be worn out."

Charlie nodded and let his hand drop to the table. Angela wondered how much longer he would be able to hang on.

"I'll go on up for a while and give you a break," said Gus, and he lifted a piece of the fresh cake from the pan and headed for the stairway.

"Bring me some coffee when the pot boils," he called back over his shoulder.

"How are you?" Angela asked as soon as Gus had gone.

Charlie looked confused over the question and Angela wondered if he had been getting any sleep.

"Thomas said you don't care for the cattle anymore."

Charlie nodded, but Angela didn't see pain in his eyes as she had expected.

"The young Stratton does that," Charlie admitted.

"Does he know how?" Angela asked before she could stop herself.

Charlie nodded a tired nod. "He's sharp enough—even though he is a city-slicker. He studies on it—and he asks if he doesn't know. I gotta hand him thet."

"Does he—does he plan to stay then? I mean—I thought—well, I just assumed that he would be going back to—to wherever, as soon as—"

Angela couldn't finish.

"Sounds to me like he means to stay," said Charlie.

Angela felt a tingle pass through her.

"And what will you do?" asked Angela.

Charlie just shrugged. "I'll figure thet out when the time comes," he replied, revealing neither concern nor enthusiasm.

"What you need is a good night's sleep," declared Angela. "Couldn't I come and stay with Mr. Stratton for a night or two and—?"

Charlie shook his head adamantly, stirring for the first time. "We make out fine—and it won't be much longer, I fear. Thet sickroom is no place fer a young lady."

"But—"

"No, ma'am," insisted Charlie, and Angela knew it was useless to argue further.

"I'd best get on home." She stood up and smoothed the skirt of her dress, feeling a little foolish now and wishing she had come over in her kitchen frock.

"Gus might like his cup of coffee now," Angela prompted.

Charlie swore softly under his breath. "I fergot all about it," he murmured, rising quickly and lifting a big mug from the cupboard shelf.

Angela let herself out and started for home deeply troubled. It was clear that Charlie was about at the breaking point. She wished there were something she could do.

She was so absorbed in her thoughts that she did not hear the approaching horse until the rider had reined in beside her.

"Good afternoon, miss."

Angela jumped in surprise.

"My apology, Miss Peterson," the young Stratton quickly

responded, stepping down from the horse with one smooth motion. "I didn't mean to startle you. Are you quite all right?" He took her hand and drew her toward him.

Angela flushed and stepped back. "Oh, I—I'm fine," she faltered. "You—you just caught me off guard for a minute. I was too deep in thought, I guess." She took another small step backward and he released her hand.

They stood there—face-to-face—assessing each other.

Angela watched his eyes move from her bonnet to her shoes and back to her face. He smiled approvingly, and she wondered if that meant she was as pretty as the city girls he knew.

Angela used the time to take a full look at the young man before her. He was even taller than she had realized. He was not dressed in the finery of their first meeting. Instead, he wore western garb—and wore it well. His clothing was newer and more expensive looking than the working clothes worn by most of the local young men. His chaps were still highly polished dark leather, his shirt unfaded from the summer sun. His wide-brimmed hat was not yet stained from rain and snow, nor his gloves hardened into the shape of curled fingers. He removed a glove and reached up to lift his hat from his head. He stood before her, dark hair glistening in the sun, dark eyes softened with concern for her welfare. Angela found him most appealing.

"I was—was just checking on your—your father—and Charlie," Angela said suddenly, taking one more step backward.

He was suddenly the young man she had met before—in spite of his change of outfit.

"I'm hurt," he said. "I was hoping you had called to see me."

Angela had regained her composure, realizing that she probably made a rather striking picture in her Sunday dress and bonnet. She turned her blue eyes directly on the young man and allowed her lips to curl into a teasing smile. "I assumed the boss would have little time for afternoon tea parties," she countered.

The young man tipped his head to one side and his eyes

studied her face. Angela felt her cheeks glow under the close scrutiny.

"I must apologize for my appearance," he said at last, "but if you will give me a few minutes, I will rid myself of the dust and filth and be happy to share that cup of tea."

He offered Angela an arm, and for one unguarded minute she was about to accept it.

"Oh, I was only teasing," she admitted. "I—I must hurry home. I've got a thousand things to do."

"What a pity!" His voice sounded as if he meant the words, but Angela still couldn't read his eyes. She felt confused, knowing that he was testing her, yet realizing she didn't understand his meaning.

"Another time then?" he asked. Angela wondered if she sensed an arrogance in the young man.

She tipped her head to one side and looked at him candidly. She was not flirting now. She had recovered from her moment of youthful foolishness. "I'll give it some thought," she replied simply. "I may call on Charlie again."

She turned to go, but he caught her arm, his grasp gentle but definite.

"And what about me?" he asked in a low voice. "What if I should wish to call?"

Angela felt her pulse racing. She hardly knew how to respond. No young man had ever asked her if he could come calling. She cocked her head as though considering—when in fact she was trying to once again gain control of her emotions.

"It hardly seems the proper time to be calling—when— when your father is so—so ill," she responded at last.

"Of course. Of course, I meant later. After he is—well again."

Angela wondered if he was very deeply concerned about his father. He didn't seem to be embarrassed that he had suggested calling when the man lay desperately ill. Nor did she believe for one minute that he expected his father ever to be well again. A shiver passed through her. She didn't think she cared much for the man, after all—even if he did think he was such a fine gentleman.

Angela eased her arm from his hold and gave him one last look. She was about to take her leave when she remembered her mama. Mama would never have allowed her children to respond to poor taste with poor taste. The young man had paid her a fine compliment and she was about to walk away in a huff. *Perhaps his city ways are different than the ways out here,* she reminded herself. *And remember, he has never really known his father. That man—sick in bed—unable to think or speak—that really has been a poor way to meet the man who should have earned his respect and love.*

Angela turned back to the young man, a friendly smile on her lips. "I do think that it is proper to attend the house of the Lord on any occasion," she said quietly. "And it would likely be quite in order for the neighbors to invite one home for dinner following."

He paused a moment as if to sort out her meaning and then nodded. "And where do I find your church?"

"It's the only one in town," she replied.

"Next Sunday?" he asked.

"Next Sunday," she nodded. "The family will be expecting you."

She turned and without a backward glance headed determinedly home.

Her cheeks burned as she walked. What had come over her? She had acted like—just like she had seen Trudie act with Thomas. She had not appreciated it in Trudie and she did not appreciate it in herself.

I refuse to act like a silly schoolgirl, she scolded herself. *If he does show up for church, then we shall all treat him as a dinner guest. But I will not—absolutely will not—flirt with him again.*

Angela's face burned even more deeply as she thought of her coy looks and teasing smiles. "Whatever came over me anyway?" she said aloud with impatience. "I have never—never acted so foolish before. I can't for the life of me imagine what I was trying to do."

Though it was still just a feeling she couldn't quite put into words, Angela was beginning to realize that buried deep within her was a young woman longing for special attention—special love.

Chapter Twelve

Sunday

Angela felt agitated as she prepared for church on Sunday morning. She should have been elated—relieved—as Thomas was, for the harvest was all in the bins and the crops had done well. Thomas was set to relax and be thankful. The family would have their needs met for another year.

Angela was thankful too. It was a relief to know that she could now shop for the needed material from which to sew winter garments. It was wonderful that they would be able to get new footwear for each family member. With thanksgiving she would buy the wool for mittens and heavy socks. But even though Angela knew she should be humming a tune of praise, she fidgeted and fiddled and felt her nerves strung tight.

She had told no one of her invitation to the young Stratton for Sunday dinner—not even Thomas. *Mr. Stratton probably won't be at church anyway*, she told herself, *and I did rather make that the stipulation.*

But just in case, Angela had two young roosters prepared and in the roasting pan and the table was set with Mama's good china.

"I see we are celebrating," said Thomas, and when Angela nodded her head, he smiled. Angela was sure that Thomas felt it quite appropriate to celebrate.

If he should happen to come—and I'm sure he won't, Angela reminded herself, *I will not act like a smitten young adolescent. I will act like the young woman Mama would expect me to be.*

99

Angela took a bit more time with her grooming, and when she finally appeared and announced that she was ready, the rest of the family was waiting for her.

"Thane's birthday gift looks nice with that dress," said Thomas approvingly as they walked out to the wagon. Angela nodded in agreement, wondering about his rather knowing smile.

It was not a long drive to church, and soon they joined the others gathering for the service.

The Merrifield brothers joined their little procession into the church, and Angela feared they were going to try to crowd in the pew beside her. With a bit of maneuvering she managed to place herself between Sara and Louise, and she smiled a polite greeting to the two young men as they passed on by.

The Andrews family was across the aisle. Angela waved a hand as discreetly as possible to signal that the lovely cameo was resting against the bodice of her pale blue calico. Mrs. Andrews smiled and Thane looked pleased.

Angela turned her attention back to the Sunday congregation.

Trudie came in with a rustle of skirts and a flip of her red hair and seated herself directly in front of the Petersons. She turned to say hello to Angela and to give Thomas a cute smile. Angela again reminded herself that she would not encourage such a manner.

The service was about to start when Trudie turned and whispered to Angela, "Look. Over there."

Angela stole a glance to the side indicated by Trudie's bobbing head, and there was the young Mr. Stratton, planted firmly in a church pew. At Angela's glance he nodded his head slightly and she felt her face flush. She turned her full attention back to the front of the church, relieved that Pastor Merrifield was taking his place behind the pulpit.

Perhaps Angela could have concentrated better on the morning service had not Trudie been so restless. Angela caught her stealing frequent glances in the direction of the young visitor. She seemed to have forgotten Thomas totally. *So that's how fickle you are, Trudie Sommers,* Angela said to herself. Then she felt anger stirring within her. *Well, if you think you can just throw Thomas aside because you have discovered a fascinating new face, you are wrong. If I have anything to do with it, Mr. Stratton will not so much as give you a "good morning."* Angela decided then and there that she might do just a bit of flirting, after all, if it would stop Trudie from claiming the attention of the young man.

From then on, Angela had a hard time paying attention to the morning worship service. She chided herself, forcing her thoughts back to what Pastor Merrifield was saying, but at another glance and toss of the red head in front of her, she would lose the train of the message again.

As soon as the service ended, Trudie was at her side. "Did you see him? Did you see him? I wonder who he is."

"You mean you don't know?" asked Angela, as though she had known the young man for years.

"Do you? Do you know him?" Trudie was shaking Angela's arm as she asked the question.

"He's our neighbor," answered Angela matter-of-factly.

"Your what?"

"Mr. Stratton," replied Angela, straightening the sleeve that Trudie had been tugging.

"Mr. Stratton? That's not him. I know Mr. Stra—You mean the son? That young man is Stratton's son?" Trudie was shrieking her whisper into Angela's ear.

"What's his name? Oh, what's his name?" Trudie demanded.

Angela suddenly realized she didn't know, but she wouldn't have admitted it for anything.

"I choose to address him as Mr. Stratton," she answered.

"Oh, you must introduce me, you simply must," Trudie gushed.

Angela stood and nodded to her sisters to allow them to exit the church.

"Very well," she said to Trudie as they walked down the aisle. "I'll introduce you if you wish."

She hoped that by the time they reached the church steps, the young man would have disappeared. But he was making

the rounds of the young men, being introduced by Thane.
Thane had met the young Stratton on more than one occasion
when he came to purchase items from the store. It seemed
that the young men of the church were giving the visitor a
warm welcome.

As Angela moved down the walk, the young man lifted his
hat and stepped forward.

"Good morning, Miss Peterson," he said politely with a dip
of his head. Angela again noticed the deep, cultured voice.

"Good morning, Mr. Stratton," she responded, almost
shyly. Feeling Trudie tug her sleeve, an impishness possessed
her. "I trust you can find your way to our dinner table with
no difficulty. We are looking forward to having you." And she
gave the young man a warm smile—almost as coy as Trudie
would have given.

There was a gasp beside her and then Trudie gave another
yank on Angela's sleeve.

"And before my friend tears my sleeve from my dress," she
went on, "let me introduce you. This is Miss Trudie Sommers.
I believe she would like to meet you."

Trudie's red face did not keep her from stepping forward
and taking the young man's extended hand.

Mr. Stratton bid her good morning. Then he turned his
attention back to Angela.

"May I drive you home, Miss Peterson?" he asked, and
Angela felt her own face flush slightly. She had not even told
Thomas they would be having a guest, and now he was pro-
posing that she ride with him instead of the family.

But Trudie was standing by, her mouth open and her eyes
wide with wonder.

"I'd like that," Angela responded. "Just give me a minute
to inform my brother," and she hastened off to find Thomas.

Thomas was talking with Thane. Angela burst in upon
them and blurted out her mission.

"Thomas," she said breathlessly, "I—I've gotten myself in
rather a—a strange situation. I invited Mr. Stratton to dinner—if he came to church first—and he is here. He has—has
asked me to ride with him, so I will see you back at the house."

Angela turned quickly without reading the two faces before her. She feared that Trudie, if left too long, might turn the tables on the day's plans.

The dinner went well enough. Thomas was courteous to their guest and spoke with him easily. Angela learned more about the young man from listening to their conversation.

He had been raised in Atlanta, his mother's hometown. In fact, he was reared in the same house that his mother had been. He had no aunts or uncles, but he did have grandparents. It sounded to Angela as if they doted on the boy.

"How did they feel about your coming west?" asked Thomas.

"They weren't very happy."

"And your mother?"

"I'm not sure my mother still claims me," he answered candidly.

"Then why did you come?"

"I had to. I had heard so many little remarks about my father over the years that I had to come and see for myself if he—if he was as they described him."

"And is he?"

"I don't know. I have been trying to piece things together. I think that many things might be accurate. But—I may never know. I still don't really know the man."

Angela felt it was a shame that his coming had been delayed until it was too late for both of them.

"Will your mother join you?"

"Oh no. She hated it out here. She would never come back."

Angela moved out of earshot. She felt like an eavesdropper in her own home. There were better ways to get to know her guest. She would wait until he volunteered the information to her.

She did discover his name. It happened as she served the coffee.

"Do you take cream or sugar, Mr. Stratton?" she asked.

"Please—please call me Carter," he quickly replied. "All of you, and I will call you Thomas, if I may," he added, asking permission from Thomas with his eyes.

Thomas nodded, and from then on they referred to their guest as Carter.

It was a pleasant afternoon. Without Trudie hovering near, Angela was able to keep her resolve of not being foolishly flirty with the young man. She acted as a proper hostess, caring for her guest and family.

When he prepared to go, Carter found a few moments with her alone.

"Will you walk me to my carriage?" he asked, and Angela realized it was the first time she had heard the conveyance referred to as a carriage. But then, perhaps his buggy was a carriage. It was certainly fancier than any other vehicle about.

She fell into step beside him and accompanied him to the hitching rail.

"This has been delightful," he assured her. "You are a much better cook than Gus," he teased, and when Angela smiled he looked pleased.

"May I come again?" he asked.

When Angela's brow began to crease he hurried on.

"I know—it doesn't look proper to call when my father is near death." His candor surprised Angela. "But we are neighbors, and I do enjoy your brother and—and the others. And I would honestly like the pleasure of your company again. May I?"

"Perhaps, as a neighbor—and friend—dropping in," said Angela, "but not as a gentleman caller—at the present."

"I understand," he said softly, and he tipped his hat and bid her good day.

Angela did not wait to see him go. She turned back to the house and her kitchen. The days were getting cooler she noticed. It was a good thing Thomas had all of the crop in the bins. Any day now they might be surprised by snow.

———

Trudie showed up on the doorstep the next day. Angela thought at first that it might be to try to make amends to Thomas for so thoroughly ignoring him the day before, but

Trudie was still full of questions about Mr. Stratton.

"Does he plan to live here?" she asked.

"I believe so," Angela replied.

"Oh-h, just think of it," crowed Trudie. "Every girl in the neighborhood will be after him, and I saw him first."

Angela wondered how Trudie came to that conclusion. She was the one who had introduced them.

"I think I'll have another party," bubbled Trudie. "I wonder what he likes to do."

"He says he likes the stage and operas," said Angela, challenging Trudie to match that with her backyard parties.

"Oh-h," Trudie sighed ecstatically, undaunted. "He is so—so sophisticated. I just love it."

Angela was glad when Trudie rose to leave. Her friend was almost to the door before she called back, "Oh, I came to see what you are wearing to the wedding on Saturday. I think I will wear my lavender satin."

Angela knew the dress. It was a lovely, full-skirted gown with generous amounts of ribbons and lace. Angela had always felt that it was not a good color choice for a person with red hair.

"I don't know," answered Angela. She had almost forgotten that Saturday was the day Hazel Conroy had chosen for her wedding. She hadn't even thought ahead to what she—or any other member of the family—would wear, but she knew they would all be expected to be there.

"I heard Hazel invite Mr. Stratton," explained Trudie, "and he said he would be delighted to attend."

Then Trudie was gone, tossing her head and smiling.

As soon as Angela had finished the morning washing, she cast a furtive look at the lowering sky and headed for the barn to find Thomas.

"Thomas," she asked, "do you mind if I drive over to Carson?"

"Today?" he questioned.

"Right now. I had forgotten about Hazel's wedding on Saturday and they have a bigger yard goods store there. I thought I could do my purchasing for the winter things we need, too."

"It's rather late in the day to be heading for Carson."

"I'll hurry. I'll have lots of time to catch the store. When the kids get home, you can put them to their choring." Then she quickly amended her words. "No, you won't need to do that. They know what they are to do."

Angela ran back to the house to prepare for the trip while Thomas hitched the horse to the light buggy.

Chapter Thirteen

The Wedding

Angela coaxed the mare into a trot and settled into the buggy for her ride to Carson. She was eager to cover the miles, but careful not to push the mare too fast. It was bumpy enough at a moderate pace and she did not want to wind the animal.

In a small box at her feet were garments from home. She had Thomas's suit to compare with others in the store. She also had one of Derek's jackets and a foot pattern for each child. She hoped these would enable her to make some sensible choices for her family and be back home again before it got too dark.

The trip took Angela longer than she had anticipated. She kept one eye on the darkening sky as she made her decisions. She did find a suit for Thomas. By comparing the old and the new she was sure that with a minor adjustment here or there, it would fit him just fine. Then she began her search for a proper suit for Derek. That took a bit longer, and Angela was really getting nervous by the time she found what she was looking for. The footwear came next—shoes and winter wear. There weren't many clothes to select from so the choice did not take long. She turned her attention to the fabric, fingering some rich materials with sensitive hands.

She found a delicately patterned calico for Sara. With a bit of lace on the collar, the finished dress surely would please the young girl. It was more difficult to make the decision for Louise. She knew her sister would like something a bit more grown-up, but Angela did not want to rush her into adult garments. Finding the right balance was difficult, but after carefully considering fabric and patterns Angela made a decision and felt pleased with her choice.

She then gave her attention to the material for her own dress. She fingered the fine silks, let the satins drip from her hand, and eyed the expensive laces with longing.

"This is foolish," she finally muttered softly. "Here I am willing to spend the autumn's harvest on a silly notion that I need to dress to attract attention. Well, I don't. I need a good sensible dress for church, not a frilly frivolous dress for partying." Angela deserted the shelves of expensive material and moved to the more durable fabrics.

In the end she chose a blue voile. It was both sensible and attractive. Then with one eye still on the darkening sky she hurried to choose materials for warm winter garments and wool yarn for mittens. Having completed her purchases, she piled them all on the counter.

The total cost was staggering, and Angela was glad Thomas had insisted she bring extra money. She paid the bill and the young man in the store helped her load her parcels into the buggy.

"Got far to go?" he asked, his eye also on the sky. Angela nodded. She had farther to go than she cared to admit.

"Looks like it could snow," the boy went on, and Angela climbed quickly into the buggy and clucked to the horse.

"Thank you for your help," she called to the boy as she turned the mare around and urged her to a trot.

The mare did not need to be encouraged. She, too, was anxious to be home again. She lifted her nose into the air and snorted, then jerked her head in impatience and headed out of town at a brisk trot.

Angela had nothing to do but hold the reins. The wind was blowing now, and she felt the sting of it right through her coat. She tucked herself in a bit more closely and turned her back slightly to the chilling breeze. She would be glad to get home.

When at last Angela pulled into the farm lane she was met

at the gate by Thomas, lantern in hand. It had long since grown dark, and she could tell by his pacing that he had been concerned.

"It took longer than I thought it would," she called to him in explanation.

"I'll take Star. You get in out of the cold," he said, relief in his voice.

Angela did not argue. She climbed stiffly down from the buggy. Derek and Louise emerged from the kitchen.

"Did you get the things?" Louise asked excitedly.

"I did," replied Angela and realized she could not speak without causing her teeth to chatter.

"You'd better get in by the fire," advised Derek. "I'll bring in these parcels."

Angela murmured her thanks and hurried into the house. Louise took her coat and hung it on its proper peg, and Angela moved to the warm kitchen stove.

"Sara, bring a chair," called Louise. "She's 'most frozen." Louise sat Angela down and poked more wood into the stove.

"Take off your shoes and stockings," she ordered as she went for the washbasin. "I'll get some warm water to soak your feet."

Louise had never taken over and told Angela what to do before, but Angela obeyed without question. For once, it felt kind of nice to be the one being fussed over.

Soon Derek came in with the parcels and the girls began to coax to see what she had bought.

"No. Let's wait until Thomas comes in," Angela said, shivering. "We'll all look at them together."

Angela was glad Thomas did not take long, though the wait was difficult for the children.

"Now you can look—one parcel at a time," Angela said as she sorted the packages, telling them who should open what.

They all seemed pleased with her purchases. Louise was especially excited over the new Sunday dress material. Angela knew the girl was envisioning herself in the pretty green print.

Thomas took the new suit to his bedroom and soon emerged

to model it. It fit him even better than Angela had hoped.

"Derek, you try on yours!" cried Sara, and Derek obliged. He came out grinning. He seemed pleased that his arm no longer showed below the hem of the jacket sleeve. The pants were a bit long. "Growing room," Angela called it and promised she'd take up the hem in plenty of time for the community wedding.

They fussed over the shoes, the warm materials, the wool— everything Angela had purchased. Angela sneezed once or twice as she thawed out beside the stove, but in spite of her discomfort she was glad she had made the trip to Carson.

They played their game again. Thomas started it spontaneously. "I remember," he began, "one time when Pa and Mama went into Carson. They came back with new clothes for each of us, but they also brought me a new bridle for Midget. Do you remember that, Angela?"

Angela nodded. It had been a long time since she had even thought of the pony Midget.

"And at the same time they brought new boots for Sara. They were so tiny. I remember thinking that I had never seen anything as little and cute as those shoes."

"Were they?" asked Sara, her eyes glowing.

"They were. Just little tiny things. Black—with buttons."

"Oh, I wish I still had them!" exclaimed Sara.

"You wore them out, if I recall properly," put in Thomas.

"Did they bring me anything?" asked Louise.

"They brought things for each of us. Let's see if I can remember some of them. Was that the time—no. It was another time they brought you the white muff. It was from Andrews' store, I think. Do you remember it, Louise?"

"The white muff? I do. I do. I remember how I loved to put my hands into it. I would take off my mittens so I could feel it on my hands. It was so soft!"

Angela sneezed again and then turned to Derek. "I remember what they brought you. That spinning top. The one you keep on your shelf. They got it for you on that trip. Do you remember?"

Derek nodded.

"Nobody could ever make it work as good as Papa," he said, and Angela realized again how much the boy missed his father.

"We'd better get Angela to bed," said Louise suddenly. Angela was surprised at the girl's concern until she added, with laughter, "If she goes and gets sick, we won't have any new dresses for the wedding."

Angela did not get sick. She worked long hours to get her sewing done. Louise and Sara even volunteered to do some of her usual chores so she could stay at the machine. At last the two suits were altered and three new dresses hung from wooden hangers, just in time for the big day.

Louise couldn't wait to appear in her new gown. She tried it on repeatedly and looked at herself in the mirror. Then she began to experiment with her hair, lifting it up this way, then holding it that way.

Oh, dear, thought Angela, *she is going to insist on wearing her hair up and she's too young for that. Now we'll have another fuss for sure.*

The weather warmed in time for the wedding. Angela was thankful for that as there really wasn't much warmth to the blue voile. There was a good deal of hurrying as they all dressed for the occasion. There was a minor fuss over Louise's hair. She came down with it pinned up in a fashion much too old for her years. Angela caught her breath and was about to comment when the unruly curls came tumbling down around Louise's ears. Louise looked as if she were about to burst into tears.

"Would you like me to help you?" offered Angela. "It is hard to get it to stay until one gets used to pinning it up."

Louise nodded, and in the re-pinning Angela was able to retain much of Louise's little girl look. At first Louise began to protest over the adjusted style but Angela cut in simply with, "This suits you better," and Louise took a second look in the mirror, grinned at her image, and said no more.

Thomas hustled them all to the buggy and headed the team for the Conroy farm.

"How is Hazel going to get everybody into the living room?" asked Sara.

"I have no idea," admitted Angela.

"Well, when I get married I'm going to pick June or July so I can have an outside wedding," went on Sara. "It's silly to try to get married in October. It could have been snowing on our heads."

"She had to wait until the harvest was over," Angela informed her sister.

"Well, there won't be any harvest to worry about in July," Sara insisted.

Thomas laughed and reached out a hand to tousle Sara's hair.

"Don't you dare," cautioned Angela. "It took me a good part of the morning to get those curls and ribbons just right."

Thomas quickly withdrew his hand and laughed again.

Trudie was the first one out to meet them when they arrived. She bounded toward them, her lavender skirts swishing over the grass. She tossed her mane of red hair and gave Thomas a coy look to see if he had taken notice of her. He was busy tethering the horses.

"He hasn't arrived yet," Trudie whispered to Angela, "but Hazel says he promised to come."

Why should Hazel care? wondered Angela. *She is about to be married.*

Trudie opened her mouth to speak again when Angela noticed Roberta. She was in her own special chair—one from which she could not fall. Angela moved toward the girl to speak to her. Trudie trailed along behind until she realized Angela's intentions.

"What if he comes?" she whispered frantically. "He'll catch you talking with her."

Angela gave Trudie a long look and moved on toward the handicapped girl.

Angela was never sure whether Roberta recognized her or just responded as she would to anyone who came near.

"Hello," Angela said.

"Hello." She held out a fragile hand, which Angela took in her own.

"How are you, Roberta?" asked Angela, giving the girl a smile.

"Haz—Haz get marry," managed the girl, pointing to the spot where a small pulpit had been set up under the trees. October or not—it was to be an outdoor wedding.

"Yes, Hazel is getting married," agreed Angela, and Roberta laughed gleefully, kicking her legs and clapping her hands.

Then Roberta turned her attention to the restraints that held her in her chair. She picked at them impatiently. "Out," she said in agitation.

"I can't take them off. You might fall," Angela tried to explain. "If you fall and get hurt, you won't see Hazel get married."

But the girl still picked at the soft straps that kept her safely in her chair.

"My, you have a pretty dress," Angela said in an effort to distract her. The dress was becoming. Angela was sure it had been sewn for this special occasion.

But Roberta would not be sidetracked. "Out," she pleaded again, and Angela was relieved when she saw Ingrid coming to bring the girl a drink and a cookie.

Just before the ceremony was about to start, Angela felt a hand touch her elbow. It was Carter. He had arrived just as he had promised. For a moment Angela wished she were wearing one of the lovely silks or satins she had admired at Carson. But the moment quickly passed. She looked across the yard to where Trudie was standing in her elaborate lavender satin. Angela couldn't help comparing her simple frock with Trudie's.

But my own simple dress suits me, thought Angela. *I am simple—not stunning like Trudie.*

Carter tipped his hat and complimented Angela with his eyes as he gazed on her new gown and her newly trimmed bonnet.

"You look lovely, Miss Peterson," he said at last, and Angela's breath caught. She wished to believe him.

"Why, thank you, sir," she responded, merriment making her blue eyes shine.

Then Angela's eyes met Thane's. He was standing as usual with Thomas. The two always managed to get together. Angela gave a little wave and smiled his way. Thane nodded in response, then returned her smile. But Angela noticed that he did not brighten as he usually did. Was something wrong? She felt her throat tighten. She wanted to ask him the reason for his serious look, but Carter was steering her to a nearby bench. Even then she might have tried to push her way through the crowd and speak with Thane for just a minute, but the preacher was taking his place at the front of the gathering. The ceremony was about to begin.

Hazel made her entrance and all eyes turned to the bride.

Chapter Fourteen

Changes

Charlie arrived at the Peterson door one evening. The wind held a chill, and Thomas quickly bid him enter and warm himself while Angela hustled to put on the coffee. One look at the poor man and she sensed something further was wrong.

"He's gone," Charlie said, lowering himself into the chair Thomas offered.

"I'm so sorry," said Angela, setting the pot on the stove and crossing to Charlie. "When?"

"This afternoon—'bout four."

"You need some sleep. You look worn out. Why don't you just stay here for the night and—?"

"No. Gus will need me."

Angela let the matter drop.

"When will the funeral be?" asked Thomas.

"We haven't made those arrangements yet—and there might be some complications."

"Complications?"

Charlie nodded his head. "The boss said, 'No service.' He just wanted to be buried on his own land. But the new boss says thet's heathen. Says there's no way he's gonna jest stick his pa in the ground without some ceremony."

Angela nodded, new respect for Carter growing in her thinking.

"Sounds reasonable to me," expressed Thomas.

Charlie nodded his head. "Well, I gotta say thet I agree

115

with 'im on thet one. Still, it's hard not to carry out the boss's wishes."

Angela laid a hand on the bent shoulder. She understood how he must feel.

"You've served him well for many years," Angela reminded him. "I guess no one could expect more than you have given."

Charlie stayed long enough to drink a cup of coffee and eat a slice of lemon loaf. Then he bundled up in his heavy coat and headed back across the empty field.

"If things had continued on as they have been, I've not sure Charlie could have taken it much longer," observed Thomas.

Angela nodded in agreement. "The poor man," she said in a whisper. "He looks like a bearded ghost. He's lost weight, Thomas, and his eyes look sunken from lack of sleep."

"Well, it's over now, I guess."

Angela nodded again and then a new thought struck her. "But not for poor Mr. Stratton," she said. "For him—there is an eternity ahead—and I fear for what it holds for him."

Thomas lifted his head to look at her.

"Oh, Thomas," admitted Angela. "I never once tried to share my faith with him."

"Pa tried," responded Thomas.

"He did?"

"More than once. I was with him one time. I remember. Pa said that the caring for the state of one's soul was the most important job a man had to do in life. Then he invited Mr. Stratton to church."

Angela waited.

"The man cursed at Pa. I will never forget it. It shocked me that a man would speak in such a way. Then he clenched his fist and shook it in Pa's face. Pa never even blinked. I was hoping Pa would punch him." Thomas stopped to smile momentarily at the memory, then went on.

"Pa didn't back down, but he allowed the man some self-respect—even though he knew he was wrong. 'Mr. Stratton,' he said. 'A man's got a right to make his own decisions in life. I'll grant you that. But I'll also continue to pray for you—and if you ever want to discuss the matter—well, you've got a neighbor and friend just over the fence.' "

"He said that?"

"I was so proud of my pa that day," declared Thomas. "I knew right then that it took a bigger man to extend his hand than it did to fight."

Angela picked up the empty coffee cups.

"Thomas," she said. "We have been so blessed—you and I—to have parents like we had. It just hurts me to think that all the—the memories that we treasure—the—the younger ones can't share. Our folks—through their teaching, built such a strong, sure base for us."

"We share them in our game and in our Memory Book."

"But that's not the same as getting them firsthand," insisted Angela.

"But it is still important," Thomas replied.

Angela crossed to the kitchen shelf that held their Memory Books. There were three scribblers now—all recording the things family members had recalled about their parents. She let her hand caress them gently. They *were* important. In sharing memories, they had grown even closer as a family.

"Yes," Angela agreed. "It's the best we can do." Then she lifted her head and spoke again to her older brother. "Thomas, we must be careful to be kind to Carter. He doesn't even have any memories of his father. Only rumors. And I don't think he and his mother are on very good terms at present, either. I could—could hear it in his voice when he spoke of her."

"I think she spoiled him—then became angry when he wanted to be his own man instead of her little boy," observed Thomas.

"Well, he needs friends. If one doesn't have family—then one needs friends even more."

————

The funeral service was held two days later. Reverend Merrifield conducted the brief ceremony, and Mr. Stratton, Sr., the community's rich man, was laid in the town cemetery with an appropriate stone marking his final resting place.

Most folks from the area attended the service. Only a few, like Mrs. Blackwell, declined.

"I had nothing to do with the man while he lived," she observed sourly, "so I see no reason to have anything to do with him when he's dead."

Mr. Blackwell came into town to get a harness repaired and slipped, unobtrusively, into the gathering.

The three mourners who stood close to the graveside made quite a contrast. Carter towered above the other two. He was dressed in a fine dark suit. His broad shoulders wore it well and his head was bowed just enough to show proper respect for the man who had been his father, but whom he had never known. The two little men who stood beside him wore the same suits they had worn for funerals over many years. The garments were faded and wrinkled—much like the two who wore them. But the faces of the two little gentlemen were etched with genuine grief. Charlie stopped to brush away a tear now and then, unaffected by the crowd of observers.

There wasn't much the Reverend Merrifield could say in comfort to the bereaved, so he spoke to those who remained behind.

"I go to prepare a place for you," he quoted and then lifted his eyes to the neighbors.

"Friends—Christ spoke those words—and so we know them to be true. He has gone to prepare a place for us—for each one of us. But for us to take advantage of His goodness—we must prepare our hearts for that place.

"Have you considered what you must do? Christ will keep His word. The place will be prepared and waiting. It will be ready when you depart this world—if you also have made preparations.

"God has told us in His Word what we must do to prepare. 'Believe on the Lord Jesus Christ and thou shalt be saved.' Repent—turn from your wickedness and unto God. Ask God to forgive those wrongs—those sins of the past—and to give you a clean heart—clean thoughts, clean actions—so that you might be prepared for the place He has prepared. Accept the forgiveness of God through the death of His Son, and be baptized in faith."

As the sermon continued, Angela stole a look at the crowd of neighbors all around the graveside. How many of them might need to hear the words being spoken? Had she really been concerned about their eternal destinies—or had she been too busy caring for her family? *Mama would have found the time—I know she would have,* Angela thought. *I must be careful so I don't get too taken up with duties that I forget people.*

Angela glanced again at the three menfolk at the grave. Carter stood respectfully, yet locked away. Angela could not read his thoughts or feelings. Charlie mourned openly. Poor little Charlie. The long illness of his boss and friend had almost done him in. Gus looked uncomfortable, as if he wished the parson would hurry. His hand supported Charlie by holding his elbow. It was touching to see the two elderly, wizened little men sharing their grief in such a manner.

"What will you do now?" Angela asked Charlie and Gus.

She had bundled up a few loaves of fresh bread in a clean kitchen towel and taken them across the field. She sat in the big kitchen. Now that Gus had been freed to return to his regular duties, he had scrubbed and polished until everything shone again.

"I guess I jest go back to my cookin'," said Gus lightly.

"And you?" asked Angela turning to Charlie. "Will you be riding again?"

Charlie shook his head slowly. "I'm too old for ridin'. Got no yen to be back out in the sun and the snow. My bones ache and the old breaks give me a twinge now and then. I guess I'll just find me a little shack somewhere and sit and rock."

Angela smiled. If anyone deserved to sit and rock, she felt Charlie did.

"Why do you need a shack? There's plenty of room here."

"Thet's what I been tellin' 'im," cut in Gus. "No reason I can see fer 'im to be lookin' fer another place. No reason."

Charlie shook his head.

"I ain't no use to nobody here anymore," he insisted. "Ain't gonna sit around an' jest get in the way."

"Why don't you come live with us?" Angela asked so suddenly that she surprised even herself.

Charlie looked up quickly to see if he had heard her right.

"We can make room," Angela continued, her mind busily trying to work out her plan.

Charlie was shaking his head slowly.

"Sure we can," she said. "I'll speak to Thomas. We'd love to have you—all of us would."

"No-o-o," spoke Charlie, but Angela was sure the idea appealed to him.

"We have a nice wide veranda that Papa built—"

"Nothing wrong with your place," cut in Charlie. "It's me. I ain't good for nothin' anymore."

"Of course you are. Don't say that. You are still worn out from your long ordeal, but you'll get your strength back again. Just wait and see. And if—if you don't—then—then we'd still like to have you."

Charlie reached out a calloused hand and patted Angela's soft young one. "You are kind, girlie—jest like yer mama. But thet arrangement wouldn't work."

"Will you at least think about it?" insisted Angela.

Charlie chuckled. "Think about it! Shucks, I'll dream about it."

Angela left feeling that with Charlie dreaming and her praying, surely something would work out.

Chapter Fifteen

A Caller

Carter caught Angela unexpectedly with his first call, and she had to excuse herself and go to her room to change and repair her hair. While she was gone, Thomas and Carter exchanged views on the weather, the year's crops, and the coming winter.

Angela returned to the kitchen quickly, and Carter turned his full attention to her.

She wanted to ask him about Charlie—but she dared not. After all, it really was none of her affair. Still, it seemed that after all his years of service to Carter's father, Charlie was due some sort of consideration.

They spent the evening in light conversation. Angela was tempted to have Thomas lay a fire in the parlor so they wouldn't have to spend all their time in the kitchen, but she withheld the suggestion. She decided to assess the situation to see if Carter was really calling on her or just paying a neighborly visit.

He was so smooth, so proper, so elegant in his plaid jacket with velvet lapels and his diamond stick-pin that Angela could not believe he could actually be interested in a simple girl like her.

Yet his eyes, his shared laughter, his absolute attentiveness—all stated that indeed he was interested. It was a puzzle to Angela—a puzzle that sent her pulse racing.

"How soon may I come again?" he asked, his eyes teasing

her as she saw him to the door. Not "may I come again" or
"would you mind?" but "how soon?" Angela held her breath
in a little gasp and looked up into the dark eyes.

"Well, I—I—" Then she smiled and tipped her head
slightly, answering in a joking mood. "April?"

"I would never last until April," he said, his eyes looking
seriously into hers.

"Then perhaps we could make it a bit sooner," she responded.

"How does Friday night sound?"

"This Friday night? This is Tuesday—that is only—"

"Three long, long days," he finished for her.

Angela took a deep breath and nodded, a smile playing
softly about her lips. "Friday night will be fine," she said in
little more than a whisper.

He nodded and turned to go, replacing his dark Stetson as
he stepped out into the chill of the night.

Angela closed the door and leaned against it. She wondered if Thomas had heard the conversation.

"I'm going up to bed," Thomas announced.

Angela realized that to Thomas, Carter's call was little
more than a neighborly visit.

"Thomas, Carter is coming again on—on Friday night."

Thomas looked up, his eyes filled with surprise.

"I was wondering—could we—could we have a fire in the
parlor? That way—should the rest of you like—like to read—
or—or whatever—in the kitchen, we won't be in one another's
way."

There! She had stated her case clearly enough. She was
being courted. She needed a bit of privacy. She fixed her eyes
on Thomas, her blood pounding through her veins.

Thomas stood quietly, just looking at her; then he reached
a hand to the chair in front of him and pushed it back against
the table. His eyes looked down at the kitchen floor as though
he were studying something. Then he swallowed. Angela
could see his Adam's apple work up and down. At last he
spoke.

"Is this what you want?"

"Why, y-yes. I—I guess it is."

"You're sure that he shares your standards? Your faith?"

"He goes to our church—almost every Sunday."

"Angela—it is more than going to church on Sunday. You know that."

She nodded. It was her turn to swallow. She twisted her hands. There were so many things about Carter that seemed so—so perfect. But she wasn't sure—not quite sure—if he actually shared her faith.

She lifted her head resolutely. "If I find that he doesn't, I can stop seeing him," she said.

"I hear it isn't always that easy," replied Thomas.

"What do you mean?"

"Well, Hazel Conroy said that about her Fred. I hear that he's already forbidden her to attend services."

That piece of news was a shock to Angela. "But Carter goes to services," she reminded her brother.

"So did Fred," Thomas answered soberly.

Angela remembered that it had been so.

"And—and what about Thane?" asked Thomas pointedly.

"Thane?"

"Thane most always comes on Friday night. Have you forgotten?"

"He can still come," she answered. "You and he can play checkers or something and—and I'll fix lunch for all of us."

Thomas looked at Angela with unbelieving eyes, shook his head sadly, then turned to the stairs.

Angela knew something was wrong. Thomas never turned his back and walked away from her. She wished to call out to him, but she closed her lips firmly. He was acting foolishly. There was no reason for him to be so upset about Carter coming to call. After all, she was an adult. She could choose her own friends.

Angela stiffened her back and lifted her chin, but she could do little about the tears that insisted on slipping out from under her long lashes.

She recalled her feelings of fear and jealousy when Thomas had seemed to enjoy the attention showered on him by Trudie.

Maybe he felt the same way now. But Angela would never leave the family. Thomas should know that. He had nothing to worry about.

Carter did call on Friday night. Thane did not. Angela missed seeing him, but quickly pushed all thoughts of him from her mind and gave her full attention to Carter.

Thomas started the fire in the parlor fireplace as Angela had requested and he also must have told the children that Angela was not to be disturbed, for no one came near the parlor door.

Angela prodded Carter gently with leading questions, hoping that he would disclose his beliefs about God. But either he did not understand her meaning or was skillful in evasion, for she never did get a satisfactory answer.

Perhaps another time, she told herself and allowed the conversation to turn to other things.

He told her about his mother. He told her of the home where he had grown up and described it so well that Angela could almost smell the sweet honeysuckle and hear the katydids.

"It must have been hard for you to leave all that," she sympathized.

"On the contrary," said Carter. "I was quite bored with it all. I wanted to come west when I was about fifteen, but Mother would not hear of it. I toyed with the idea for years before I finally found the resolve to actually do it. Mother was dead set against it, you see. At first I hoped I could change her mind. But that didn't work. Finally we had a big quarrel. I'm sorry it had to happen in that way—but I'm not one bit sorry I came."

He reached down to take the small hand that rested on the sofa between them, and Angela flushed slightly. Courting was all new to her, and she was not good at knowing what to say and how to say it. She was quite sure Trudie would have had a ready response—and would have invited another compliment. But Angela sat tongue-tied.

Carter studied the small hand he held in both of his own. "How do you keep them so soft—when you work so hard?" he asked.

Angela was flustered again. She wasn't sure if she was supposed to answer the question or if it was just a flattering remark. She let it go.

"You should have someone waiting on you—rather than you doing all of the caring for others," he continued.

"I—I like to care for others," she stammered.

"I know you do." His eyes held hers. She knew he was paying her tribute. "You are the most sincerely selfless little creature I have ever met. Any man would be honored to get such tender care."

Angela wasn't sure she understood the full meaning of his words, but she was sure he intended them as a verbal caress. She withdrew her hand slowly and took a deep breath. "Perhaps I should see to refreshments," she offered, rising before he could object.

She was surprised when she reached the kitchen to discover the lateness of the hour. There was no one at the table or in the big chair beside the stove.

"Oh my!" she exclaimed. "They must all be in bed. I wonder if they had their milk and cookies?"

Angela took her time in preparing the serving tray and arranging the coffee cups. She needed to calm her nerves and to think soberly.

By the time she returned to the parlor, she was in control again. She took over the role of hostess easily and efficiently. She was even charming, without being forward.

After his third cup of coffee, Carter withdrew his pocket watch and looked shocked as he read the time.

"My word!" he exclaimed. "Where have the hours gone? You see the effect you have on me, Angela. I lose all track of time and place."

"It has gone quickly, but we had much to talk about," Angela said as she began to gather the lunch things and place them back on the tray.

"Yes," agreed Carter, his eyes serious as they studied her.

"We have had. And so much more that we haven't yet discussed. I'm afraid I will have to insist that you allow me more of your time, sweet Angela." His eyes and voice were teasing again. Angela felt that she knew better how to respond when he was in a light mood.

"Well—maybe just a teeny, weeny bit of time," she said, indicating a small amount with her thumb and finger. She laughed softly and he smiled his slow, deliberate smile.

"And when might that teeny, weeny bit be available?" he asked her.

"Well—"

"And please don't tell me April," he said with a mock groan.

"What would you like me to say?" asked Angela coyly.

"How about tomorrow?"

She hoped he was teasing again.

"Saturday evening is always family time," she answered quickly.

"Could I take you to dinner on Sunday—somewhere? Where does one go for a fancy dinner around here?"

"One does not go for a fancy dinner around here," Angela laughed. "One could get a beef and potato meal at the hotel. But not on Sunday. And not me. I always prepare a special dinner for the family on Sunday."

She didn't tell him about their game and the Memory Book.

"See!" he pointed out. "It is like I said. You are always more concerned about others than you are about yourself."

"But I—"

He reached out to lay the tip of his finger on her lips, and she stopped protesting mid-sentence.

"When may I see you again?" he asked. "I really don't want to wait very long."

Angela raised a hand to remove his finger from her lips. His hand closed quickly over her own. She felt confused—crowded—unable to think straight. "Why don't we talk about it on Sunday—after church?" she suggested.

He seemed disappointed, but he accepted her arrangement.

"Until Sunday then," he confirmed and reached for the hat he had left lying on the sofa table.

Chapter Sixteen

The Will

Angela decided that Carter could call again on Tuesday. She felt it was a bit soon, but she could not turn down his pleading dark eyes.

They also had another caller on Monday. Charlie braved the weather to make his way across the field.

He sipped coffee, savored chocolate cake, and talked of neighborhood events until after the three younger children had been sent to bed. Then with just Thomas and Angela sharing the table, he brought up what he had really come to talk about.

"They read the will today."

For a moment Angela did not catch the meaning of his words.

"Mr. Stratton was wise to have drawn a will," commented Thomas, and Angela understood.

Charlie nodded.

They sat in silence for a minute. Thomas and Angela both sensed there was more on Charlie's mind.

"It held some surprises?" prompted Thomas.

"It did."

Charlie pulled a yellowed envelope from his pocket. On the front in scrawling handwriting was the name of Karl Peterson.

"Papa!" said Angela in surprise.

Charlie nodded.

"But Papa has been gone for—" began Angela.

"The boss must have written this letter before yer pa died—an' then forgot about it bein' in thet drawer with his will," responded Charlie.

Thomas took the envelope and turned it over and over in his hands.

"Why don't you open it?" advised Charlie.

Thomas carefully tore a corner off the envelope and slit the edge. He withdrew a short letter in the same scrawling script that appeared on the envelope.

"Dear Karl," Thomas read aloud. "I might not have been much of a neighbor over the years. I've been bitter about many things, but I see now that much of it was my own doing. If anything should unexpectedly happen to me, I just wanted you to know that I've been thinking on what you said. It does make a lot of sense. I don't know which way I will decide, but you have done your part. I admire a man with guts enough to speak his mind on what he believes."

It was signed simply, "Carter."

"Carter was named after his pa?" asked Angela in surprise.

Charlie nodded. "She did do the man that small favor," he admitted, speaking of the former Mrs. Stratton.

"Does Carter know this?" asked Angela.

"About the letter—or about the name?"

"Well—well, both. I mean, it must be—be special to him to share his father's name. And the—the letter. Why, what if—what if Mr. Stratton did think on the things Papa said? What if he did decide to ask forgiveness for all of those things from his past?"

Angela felt sudden excitement. Wouldn't it be wonderful if the man had made his peace with God?

But Charlie was not finished with his surprises.

"The boss named Gus an' me in the will," he said, and his voice broke.

Both Angela and Thomas looked up. The little man was fighting to control his emotions. He nodded and blinked hard, not wanting to allow tears.

"He left Gus three thousand dollars."

Angela caught her breath. It was impossible to imagine that much money.

"What does Gus plan to do?" she asked when she could speak again.

"He don't know. It caught him off guard. He says he ain't got no call fer the money. But I 'spect he'll find some way to spend it."

Charlie managed a smile.

"And you—?" prompted Thomas.

"He left me the parcel of land on the crick an' the little cabin thet sits on it."

"Oh, Charlie!" squealed Angela, and she threw her arms around his neck. "That's—wonderful. You'll have a place of your very own. You can just—just sit and rock—or fish or just do nothing."

Charlie was grinning. "I always had a feelin' fer thet little cabin," he admitted when Angela stopped squeezing and stepped back. "I guess the boss knew how I felt."

Then Charlie went on. "He left me a thousand dollars, too. Now I don't need to worry none about a grub-stake."

"Oh, that's wonderful! Just wonderful!" Angela exclaimed again.

Thomas reached over to pat the old man on the back.

"Well, I dunno," said Charlie hesitantly. "The new boss don't think it's so great."

"What do you mean?" asked Angela, a frown creasing her brow.

"Oh, he don't care none about the money. Got enough left anyway, I guess. His pa did leave him the rest of what he owned. But he don't cotton none to losing thet crick bottom. Says it's the best cattle piece he's got."

Angela's eyes shadowed with emotion. She felt bad for Carter. It didn't seem quite fair that a son should lose his property to an employee. But surely with all of the land he had now, he wouldn't need the bit that had been left to Charlie.

"Doesn't he have access to water on the rest of his land?" asked Thomas.

"Oh, shore. Shore," said Charlie. "Lotsa water. But I guess he took a fancy to thet piece, too."

Thomas shook his head slowly. "Well, it's too bad," he acknowledged, "but I guess a will is a will."

Charlie shook his head slowly. "Not really," he told them. "Shore it says in the will thet it's mine—but thet don't always hold, I guess."

"You mean—?"

"I mean the lawyer fella says thet even a proper will can be contested."

"Contested?"

"Yeah—taken to court to see if it is legally bindin'—or can be overturned."

"Who could do that?" asked Angela, shocked.

"The fella who thinks he has right to it," responded Charlie.

"Carter?" asked Thomas.

"Not Carter," objected Angela quickly.

But Charlie was nodding his head. "Told me straight out that he plans to go to court and get his property back," said Charlie. The mere mention of a court battle made him look tired and old.

"But you said—" began Angela.

"Shore. The will says it's mine. Carter says it's his." Charlie's eyes were coming to life. Angela saw the snap in them. The old man raised his head and his stubborn chin lifted slightly.

"So what do you plan to do?" asked Thomas.

"Fight it!" snapped Charlie. "I'm not gonna jest hand it on over to 'im. The boss gave it to me. I'm gonna fight it."

Angela felt a sickness begin to creep through her body. She had to sit down in the nearest chair.

Oh, dear God, she prayed silently. *And we—I—will be caught right in the middle.*

Angela longed to discuss the situation with Carter the next evening, but she didn't feel the freedom to bring up such a sensitive subject. They talked of other things. Little things. Funny things. Things from their different backgrounds.

Carter did not even mention the will, and Angela was sure he was unaware they had any knowledge of its contents.

Thane would say just what he was thinking and feeling, Angela thought, and then checked herself. *What does Thane have to do with this? Why did I make that comparison?*

Angela quickly returned her thoughts to what Carter was saying. He was full of plans for the ranch, the house, and somehow Angela knew he expected her to be excited, to share his dreams.

"It sounds wonderful," she put in when Carter stopped for a breath.

"It will be," he said with confidence. "I am going back to Atlanta to do my shopping. I know the stores there and can get just what I want."

"How will you ever carry it all back out here?" asked Angela innocently.

"I'll ship it by rail. Shouldn't take too long. I figure by next spring—or summer at the latest—the house should have a whole new look."

"I think it's charming as it is," said Angela.

"Wait until you see what I'm going to do—you'll love it."

Angela had a strange thought—and the courage to voice it. "Does it really matter if I love it?"

Carter looked surprised. He opened his mouth to comment, but Angela quickly continued.

"I'm sure that your good taste will show throughout your lovely house," she smiled, "but what if I—what if I don't have the good sense to like the same things you do?"

For a moment he appeared surprised, but then he looked at her as if she must be teasing. He smiled, though his eyes did not lighten, and he spoke in bantering fashion, "Well, then—I guess we just throw it all out and start over," he said with a laugh, but Angela wasn't convinced.

When he left he promised that he would see her on Friday night, and Angela moved to the kitchen to wash the dishes.

She was still troubled as she prepared for bed and tucked herself in under the snug quilt made by her mother's hands.

"Oh, God," she prayed earnestly, "I wish I had my mama

now. I need her so. I just know if she were here she'd be able to help me sort this all out."

Angela finally fell into a restless sleep.

Carter did not come on Friday night. He stopped by on Wednesday to inform Angela that he would be out of town for several days. He promised to come over the minute he returned, then surprised her by pulling her gently forward and kissing her on the forehead.

Angela felt sure the trip had something to do with his father's will. In the afternoon she bundled up against the cold wind and headed across the field to the big house. She didn't have baking to take along, but Gus was back in his own kitchen so he no longer needed her cooking.

She was welcomed by both Gus and Charlie. Angela was not surprised by this until Gus inadvertently mentioned that he missed Charlie since he no longer lived at the ranch house.

"You don't live here?" exclaimed Angela. "Where do you live?"

"I moved into my little shack," said Charlie with satisfaction.

"Is it warm enough?" Angela asked, thinking of the cold winter winds and the driving snow.

"Sure is," said Charlie proudly. "It's as snug as a nest in there—and lots of good wood piled up at the back, too."

Angela was relieved. "So how come you're here?" she asked.

"Oh, I still sneak over for a cup of coffee now and then when I know Gus will be alone."

"You knew?"

"We have us a little signal system worked out," he said with a grin, and Gus winked at Angela.

Angela did not ask them to reveal their secret.

"We sure do. We sure do," Gus chuckled.

"Then you know that Carter has gone to the city—and why?"

Charlie nodded. "He's settin' the wheels in motion for the trial over the will. Wants him the best lawyer he can find for the case."

Angela nodded slowly. She had feared that was the reason. "And you?" she asked Charlie.

"Figured I'd be my own defense," Charlie told her. "Me and thet there piece of paper thet says the land is mine."

"But—?" began Angela.

" 'Course I got me a piece of advice from ol' Ed Stern. He said thet possession is nine-tenths of the law, or somethin' like thet. Advised me to move right in without hesitation."

Angela nodded. The pieces were falling together.

"And, I was anxious to move anyway. Nothin' fer me to do here but hassle Gus."

The twinkle had returned to Charlie's eyes.

"How will you get supplies?" asked Angela.

"Neighbors been right good about it."

Angela knew that the Conroys and Blackwells lived in the direction of Charlie's shack. Before she could make further comment, Charlie went on.

"Ol' man Blackwell is a rather decent sort. An' him tied to thet woman fer all these years. Don't know how the man has stood it. Sneaks over every now and then fer a bit of chin-wag or a cup of strong coffee. He popped in on the way to town an' says he will do thet whenever he's goin' by."

Angela smiled. It was good that the two men had each other. "Do you have any idea when—when this trial might come up?" asked Angela. She felt far more free to talk to Gus and Charlie than she did to Carter, but she did not stop to analyze the reason.

"Carter would like it all done up before Christmas," said Charlie, "but Ed Stern says those things can sometimes take a good while."

Angela nodded. It really wasn't long until Christmas.

"Well, I'd better be getting home," she said, pushing back her cup and getting to her feet. "Thank you, Gus, for the coffee."

"You're welcome," said Gus. "Anytime. Anytime."

"Come over when you can," Angela invited, her words directed to both men but her eyes resting on Charlie.

"Well, now, I reckon I would need to know the time fer

thet," said Charlie, who had always just dropped over in the past. "I hear me through the locals' report thet you sometimes have a caller."

Angela reddened. "But that doesn't mean—" she began.

" 'Course not," said Charlie. "Jest a bit uncomfortable, if you know what I mean."

"You can come any Saturday night or Sunday afternoon," Angela informed him and then promised herself she would be sure not to invite Carter on those days.

———

The hearing was set for January 15. Carter did not speak of it to Angela. She heard it from Charlie. She admitted to herself that she was a bit hurt that Carter had not discussed it with her. But perhaps he wanted to spare her feelings, knowing how she cared for Charlie.

Angela decided to push the whole matter aside and concentrate on preparations for Christmas.

Chapter Seventeen

Christmas

Angela went to town to do some shopping. She hadn't seen the Andrewses, except at church, for what seemed ages. She decided to leave a little visiting time in her schedule.

Mrs. Andrews greeted her warmly, as always, and ushered her into their living quarters behind the store.

"How are things going, dear?" the woman asked as she pushed the teakettle forward over the heat of the firebox.

"Fine—I guess," said Angela as she removed her heavy coat and placed it on the back of a chair.

"We hear you have been entertaining Mr. Stratton," Mrs. Andrews said openly.

"Yes," admitted Angela. "He calls." She felt she should be making her announcement with a gleam in her eyes and excitement in her voice. She was aware that there was neither.

"Ma Andrews," Angela began, calling the woman by the name she had used for many years, "have you heard about the trial?"

"I guess everyone around has heard of the trial," the woman answered.

"Well, do you think—do you suppose there is any danger of Charlie losing his land and cabin?"

"I really couldn't say, dear. I have no knowledge of legal things, but most folks are saying that Charlie has a fairly good case."

Angela wasn't sure that was good enough, but she held her

137

tongue. It would be such a shame if Charlie were to lose his small cabin.

Mrs. Andrews asked, "What does Carter say—?"

"We haven't talked about it," Angela answered quickly.

"I see," said Mrs. Andrews as she poured the tea.

The conversation turned to Christmas. "I've been hoping you would get to town," Mrs. Andrews said. "I wanted to check to be sure you and the family are planning to have Christmas dinner with us."

"Oh yes," responded Angela before she even had time to think. The Peterson family had shared Christmas dinner with the Andrews family ever since their mother had passed away.

Then Angela thought of Carter. Was he expecting an invitation to the Petersons'? Well, she would just explain to him the long-standing tradition. She couldn't very well invite him to accompany them. Could she? She glanced up at the kind woman who was pouring the tea and was about to blurt out her request when she thought better of it. Carter hardly knew the Andrewses, whereas she had thought of them as family for a number of years. Certainly Carter would not feel comfortable in such circumstances.

They talked further of Christmas and of the church Christmas pageant and the costumes Angela needed to prepare for Louise and Sara. Derek had announced quite forthrightly that he was too big to take part in the Christmas drama now. Angela had not argued. She was pleased to have Derek showing a mind of his own.

"Will Louise be wearing her hair up this year?" Mrs. Andrews asked. "Agnes has talked of nothing else for the past several months. Especially since she saw Louise at Hazel's wedding."

Angela looked at the older woman. "What do you think Mama would do?" she asked. "I don't want to be fighting Louise all the time, but she is constantly pressing me to let her do this and let her do that. I really don't know the proper time for these—these various things of—of youth."

Mrs. Andrews smiled. "Do you remember when you went through it?" she asked.

Angela shook her head slowly.

"Well, I do. Your mama handled you so wisely. 'Yes,' she said, 'you may have your hair up just as soon as you take over the chore of baking bread. A lady should never make bread with her hair hanging loose about her face.'"

Angela did remember then. She had been only eleven when she had begun to pester her mama about putting up her hair. She flushed slightly.

"I remember. I was even younger than Louise," she admitted.

"Yes, but you put it off for another two years after your mama's little talk."

"I was thirteen—and I had to take over baking the bread. Mama was much too ill."

Mrs. Andrews nodded solemnly, remembering the young child who had been forced into an adult role.

"Well, then, I guess, if it's all right with you, Louise and Agnes will wear their hair up this year," said Angela.

Mrs. Andrews agreed with a hearty laugh. "We will have two happy girls when we tell them."

Angela looked at the clock. "Oh, dear. I must hurry or I won't be home in time to make supper." She picked up her coat, hugged Mrs. Andrews, and hurried through the door into the store.

Thane was there waiting on a customer. Angela hung back until he had finished and then approached him. She had not seen him for several weeks, other than at church. She greeted him warmly.

"Hello. I guess your father is keeping you busier than ever. We've missed you."

Thane smiled, but Angela thought she saw sadness in his eyes. It reminded her of the look on his face at Hazel's wedding.

"Is something wrong?" she asked softly, drawing closer to the young man.

"I'm not sure," he responded. "Are you happy?"

Angela was taken by surprise at his question. "Well, yes— I guess."

"Then I'm happy," he said, and this time he gave her a full smile and a chuck under the chin. "How's Tom?"

Angela answered that Thomas was just fine—but missing their Friday night checker game.

"I hear you have other company on Friday night," Thane said frankly.

Angela flushed slightly but quickly recovered. "Well, that doesn't mean there isn't room for old friends."

"Well—room maybe—but it might be a little—uncomfortable. All those people crowded into one kitchen."

"Oh no!" exclaimed Angela. "Carter and I use the parlor."

The sad look returned to Thane's eyes. "You need some groceries?" he asked as he turned to the shelves behind him. Angela laid her list on the counter.

Carter did not look happy when Angela explained their Christmas arrangements.

"I was counting on us being together," he said, his dark eyes shadowed.

"But we have always gone to the Andrewses'," Angela explained. "Ever since Mama died. The family would be heartbroken if I suggested something else."

"Why don't you let them go and you and I make our own plans?" he suggested.

"Be separated on Christmas?" Angela couldn't believe her ears.

"Well, you won't always be together. Perhaps now is a good time—"

"There is never a good time to break up a family," Angela said firmly, surprised at her fervor.

He nodded reluctantly. "Fine," he said but his voice held disappointment. "Then how do we get a bit of Christmas?"

"Could you come over Christmas Eve? We'd love to have you join us. We always exchange our gifts and read the Christmas story and discuss our memories of other Christmases. Then we have popcorn and pull taffy and—"

"Angela," cut in Carter, "I meant just the two of us."

Angela bit her lip. She had not even thought of it being just the two of them. "I'm sorry," she said, "but I don't think I can do that. It's important for us to all be together on Christmas."

Carter looked upset but he still pressed. "What about the evening of Christmas Day?"

"We always stay late at the Andrewses', and if the weather is nice we go for a sleigh ride."

"The evening before Christmas Eve?"

Angela thought about that. There was no reason Carter couldn't come calling on the twenty-third.

"That would be fine," she agreed and gave him one of her smiles.

The days slipped by quickly and Angela scarcely had time to finish her baking and her gift-making before Christmas was upon them. She had seen Carter twice a week in the intervening time and he always made special mention of the evening of the twenty-third. Angela felt that he was gently reminding her that she had put her family before him, but she held firm and gave him a smile whenever he mentioned the coming evening.

He still had not discussed the trial, and Angela did not have the courage to bring up the subject.

When the twenty-third arrived Angela dressed carefully in her blue voile. She had not worn it since Hazel's wedding. She smoothed the skirt over her slender frame and studied herself in the mirror. The dress, in its very simplicity, did become her. She turned to the task of pinning up her hair, leaving little tendrils to gently curl against her cheeks. Then she fastened Thane's cameo about her neck and looked again at the total picture.

"Well," she said to her reflection, "that's about as good as it's going to get. I can't do much more." And so saying, Angela went downstairs to make sure the parlor fire had been lit and that the refreshments were ready for later.

Carter came promptly at eight. Angela ushered him inside, noting the cold gust of air that accompanied him.

"It's dreadful out there!" she gasped. "What a horrible night to be out."

Carter laughed and allowed her to take his heavy coat and his hat. Angela hung them up while he greeted the other family members.

Then she beckoned him to the parlor. "Come in and warm yourself by the fire," she invited, and he followed her into the room.

"It is cozy in here," he observed as he seated himself on the sofa. Angela moved to place another log on the cracking flames.

"Come," he invited. "Sit here beside me and we'll enjoy the fire together."

Angela accepted his invitation.

"Now," he said taking her hand in both of his, "tell me what you have been doing to get ready for Christmas."

Angela felt that it would be a rather boring account so she countered, "Most of my time has been in the kitchen. You tell me what you have been doing instead."

"Well—I made another trip to the city," he offered.

Angela noted the gleam in his eyes. "Business?" she asked.

"No. Pleasure," he answered, and he lifted her hand and placed a kiss on her fingers, studying her carefully as he did so.

Angela did not withdraw her hand—nor did she flush with embarrassment.

"I think that if I ever went to the city it would be for pleasure also."

"You have never been to the city?" he asked.

Angela shook her head.

"Then we must right that," he said, kissing her fingers again.

"So-o," said Angela. "Are you going to tell me all about your pleasurable trip?"

His dark eyes flashed. "I'd love to," he said, so softly that she barely caught his words. "I went to the city shopping—

just in case a certain lovely lady I know accepts my offer of marriage."

Angela's eyes widened and her breath caught in her throat. She almost withdrew her hand.

"Well," he prompted. "Do you? Will you?"

"Are you—?" began Angela.

"I am asking you to be my wife."

"But I—I never dreamed—"

Angela stopped short. She had dreamed. Well, sort of. But she had not really prepared herself for anything like this. This seemed so soon. So sudden. So unreal.

He pulled her close and kissed her cheek, letting his lips brush her hair and linger near her ear.

"Will you, Angela?" he asked again. "I am still waiting for your answer."

Angela pulled back and looked into his eyes. She lifted a hand to touch his cheek.

"Are you sure?"

"I am sure," he whispered.

"But—but don't you think it's too soon? Have we known each other long enough? Do we know each other well enough?"

"Angela, I know all I need to know about you. You are the sweetest, most caring, most unselfish woman I have ever met. And on top of that, you are lovely to look at. What more could any man want? What could we possibly gain by waiting? Please, don't put me through that agony. I need you with me."

"Oh, Carter, I do so want to do the right thing. I do want to make you happy." She stared into his dark eyes. "Yes, yes, I will marry you. I will be happy to be your wife."

He pulled her close and kissed her. Angela had never been kissed in such a way before. She felt the blood rushing through her body, pounding at her temples. For a moment she felt faint.

So this is how it is to be in love, she thought, and she lifted her lips so he might kiss her again.

I'm getting married. I'm getting married, her heart sang. *Oh, if only Mama were here now.*

Chapter Eighteen

News

It wasn't until morning came that Angela realized the seriousness of her commitment. She was about to announce her good news at the breakfast table, but when her eyes traveled from one face to another she bit her tongue. Thomas was impatient to get off to town before the weather had a chance to delay him. He had a hog to sell, and the price he got would determine the kind of Christmas the family would be celebrating. Derek, Louise and Sara were riding along into town to do their own Christmas shopping.

Louise fussed as she dished out the porridge. Her hair had not cooperated when she pinned it up. It looked precarious to Angela even now, in spite of the many combs attempting to hold it.

Derek was quiet again. Angela had told herself that he was gradually coming out of his shell, but on this particular morning he seemed withdrawn. Angela felt herself tensing up as she looked at him.

Sara bubbled as usual, completely oblivious to the moods of those about her. Her whole little body bounced as she went about her morning task of setting the breakfast table. And while she bounced, she talked—a steady stream that seemed to get on Louise's nerves even more than usual.

"Sara, why can't you ever be quiet?" Louise demanded at last, flipping her head impatiently.

It was the wrong thing for her to do. Rolls of hair came

tumbling down about her ears, causing Thomas to snicker in spite of himself. With a wail, Louise headed for her bedroom, hair streaking out behind her as she fled.

Angela gave Thomas a look of reproach, then retracted it with the hint of a smile. Louise did look pretty funny.

Sara stopped her chatter long enough to look from Thomas to Angela and back again, her eyes asking what would happen next.

Angela finished serving the porridge and then quietly slipped from the room to see if she could get Louise, and her unruly hair, back under control.

Now is definitely not the time to share my good news, she decided as she headed for the bedroom and the sound of sobs.

"Louise." She spoke softly as she approached the distraught girl. "Louise?"

The only response was louder wailing.

"Louise." Angela tried again, sitting on the edge of the bed and brushing back the tangled hair. "Don't get your eyes all red and swollen. I can fix your hair, but I can't do much to help puffy eyes."

Louise seemed to be considering the comment, for her crying diminished some.

"Come. I'll try pinning it. Hair can be terribly obstinate— until it gets used to being up. Let me see if I can fix it for you."

"I'm not going to town," wailed Louise.

Angela sat in silence for a moment and then responded with a firmness that surprised even herself. "Oh yes you are. You still haven't done your shopping. And if you don't, it will spoil everyone's Christmas. A few locks of unruly hair are not going to keep you from it. Now, get yourself up. You'll be mussing your dress."

Angela took the girl's arm and gave it a gentle tug.

"But, Angela," protested Louise, "my eyes are already red and swollen."

Angela could not be so easily put off. "You have a long ride ahead—and it is sharp this morning—with a brisk wind. By the time you get there, your eyes will be back to normal—or else red and stinging like everyone else's."

Louise hoisted herself up on her elbows and gave Angela a disdainful look.

"Right now," Angela said sharply. "You are making the others late."

Louise arose and settled herself at her vanity but refused to pick up her mirror or give Angela directions as to how she wished her hair pinned.

Angela tried to ignore the pouting girl. She swept the thick hair back with the stout brush and gathered it neatly together in the palm of her hand. Then she began to twist and lift, pinning as she went. In a few moments the task had been completed and Louise couldn't resist just a tiny peek in the mirror.

She made no comment, but Angela caught the flash of satisfaction that crossed her sister's face before she could hide it.

"Now—mop up your face and come for your breakfast," Angela said. "The rest will have finished by the time we get there."

Louise was not the only one who avoided eye contact when the two returned to the kitchen. Angela was afraid that if she observed a twinkle in Thomas's eyes she might not be able to hide a titter of her own. Nor did Angela want the incident to trouble Derek further. And Sara would be watching for the tension to ease so she could resume her chatter, and Angela wasn't quite ready to listen to more prattle about incidental things.

So Angela crossed to the stove, brought back the bowls of porridge meant for her and her younger sister, and settled herself at the table without lifting her eyes.

The others had finished. Angela gave a slight nod to recognize the fact and then said, as softly as her tense throat would allow, "You may all be excused."

"But we haven't had our morning Bible story," objected Sara, and Angela's eyes did lift then. She looked quickly at Thomas who sat, Bible in hand.

"So we haven't," she admitted, a flush touching her cheeks. Then her look turned to one of beseeching. "We are late," she said simply. "Perhaps this once you could read while we eat."

Thomas nodded and began the morning reading. By the time he was ready for prayer, Angela and Louise had finished their porridge and were sitting with hands neatly folded in their laps. They prayed together.

After the door had closed on the four family members, Angela dropped back into a kitchen chair, coffee cup before her. *What will Carter think of all of this?* was her first thought. *Well, he did ask me to marry him. I didn't just dream it,* she reminded herself, and then another thought quickly followed. *It's going to be so—so wonderful to have someone to share the responsibility of caring for the family. I know I have always had Thomas—but he can go now—go away to do the work he has always dreamed of. He will be so happy—*

Tears formed in Angela's eyes. She would miss Thomas. They had been so close. Had worked together for so many years as a team, raising their younger siblings.

She brushed impatiently at the unbidden tears. "Here I am, on the happiest day of my life, sobbing like a buffoon," she scolded herself. "Why, I should be singing my way through the morning chores—and here I sit crying in my coffee."

Angela decided not to drink the second cup of coffee, after all. She took the cup to the slop pail and poured out the contents, then turned her attention to the morning dishes.

"It is just that the morning did not start out well," she informed herself. "Things will soon be right again."

She cast a worried look toward the kitchen window. The sky had darkened and a stiff wind was blowing.

I do hope Thomas makes it to town and back before it storms. And I hope the children are bundled up warmly enough against the wind. I wonder if Louise wore her muffler. She is getting so full of silliness that she'd rather freeze than be thought out-of-style. Oh, dear! What will I ever do with the girl?

Angela's mind turned to prayer. "Lord, you know how hard it is to be growing up. And Louise seems to be having a particularly bad time with it. How can I help her, Lord? Mama would have known just what to do and say—but I stumble along and make so many blunders. Give me wisdom, Lord.

Give me wisdom. With Louise. And with Sara. Give me patience with her constant chattering, too, Lord. And with Derek and his buried grief. Help me, Lord. And help me to pick the right time to share with them the news that I am to marry. May they be just as excited about a new home as—as I will be—as I am."

Angela did not say Amen. She knew her prayer might be taken up again many times throughout her day.

In the afternoon, Angela was surprised to see Thane. He had been out their way delivering groceries to the Widow Thorson and had decided to drop in, he said. Angela pushed the kettle forward and prepared a cup of hot lemonade to help take the chill from his bones.

They chatted and laughed as old friends. Then he said he must get home since the day before Christmas was always a busy one in the store. As he left, Angela called after him that she would be seeing them all on the day following, and he called back that he hoped it wouldn't storm and prevent them. Angela turned again to her preparations for the family evening.

The family arrived home in a flurry of excitement and much laughing and bantering as they headed for bedrooms to wrap gifts before the evening gift exchange. Angela called out orders as to chores to be done before supper. The girls responded good-naturedly, but Derek was still quiet and withdrawn. Angela was relieved that Louise had returned to good humor—probably something to do with the fact that she had been given a nice compliment on her hair by Claude Sommers. Sara shared the news and, though Louise shrieked and scolded, Angela was sure Louise was secretly pleased that Sara had told.

The stock was cared for, the woodbox stacked high, and extra water carried from the well before they gathered around the kitchen table, where the lamp cast a soft glow on wind-chilled faces and the kitchen stove sent out waves of warmth.

Angela looked at the little circle of family. Everyone was

relieved to be in out of the cold and most anxious for the evening's festivities—simple as they were.

Angela had taken special care with the meal. The chicken was fried just the way Thomas liked it. The biscuits were high and fluffy. The peas had been creamed to suit Sara, and there was cranberry sauce to please Louise. The fruit cake was especially for Derek.

"Are we having company?" asked Derek, casting a furtive glance about.

Angela laughed. "Who would come out on a night like this?" she asked, and Derek just shrugged his slim shoulders and looked relieved.

"Thane used to," put in Sara.

A hush fell on the room and all eyes turned to Angela.

"Why doesn't he come anymore?" went on Sara, wistfulness in her voice.

"Why, he comes. He stopped by for a few minutes today."

Angela thought she saw a smile play about the corners of Thomas's mouth, but he made no comment.

Sara did not let it pass. "He did? And I didn't see him," she mourned. Then she went on. "But he doesn't come much. He used to come—lots and lots. Why doesn't he do that anymore?"

"I—I don't know. He's—he's been very busy helping his father expand the store, I guess," said Angela. "He says they are finally done with it. He'll have more time now."

"I miss him," continued Sara. "I haven't had any lemon drops for—for just years."

"Sara!" Angela scolded. "I hope that Thane means more to you than lemon drops."

Sara fidgeted in her seat, but Derek raised his eyes to Angela's.

She could feel a probing, a questioning, and she wondered what he was thinking. She felt like squirming under his gaze, yet didn't know why. To Angela's relief he dropped his eyes to his plate.

"Did you fight?" asked Louise bluntly.

"Who?" asked Angela, knowing full well whom she meant.

"You. You and Thane."

"Of course not! What do you mean? Why would Thane and I fight?"

"Well, he used to come see you all the time and he doesn't anymore," said Louise with a shrug.

"He—he didn't come to see me. He—he came to see us—all of us," Angela protested, her cheeks flushing.

"Oh no," denied the chattery Sara. "He used to come to see you. I know. I saw him looking at you."

"Don't talk foolish," Angela hushed Sara as she rose to replenish the chicken platter that was still piled high.

She had planned to share her proposal with the family over the supper table, but now did not seem like a good time to declare her news.

"Sara, that's enough chatter," Thomas said softly. "Stop your talking and clean up your plate or we'll all need to sit and wait for you."

Angela noticed that each family member still had a full plate. Sara was no slower that the rest of them, yet she felt thankful that Thomas had put a stop to the conversation.

"What is it?" Thomas asked when the two of them sat alone at the kitchen table sharing the warmth of the stove and the dim light of the lamp. The taffy-pulling and popcorn-making was over for another year and each gift had been exchanged and received with proper fuss and appreciation. The three younger children had been sent off to bed, with Angela and Thomas left to clean up the kitchen and then catch their breath.

Angela raised her head.

"You've got something on your mind," Thomas continued.

Angela did not deny it. It would be wrong—and foolish—for her to do so.

"I—I had a proposal for marriage," she answered, trying hard to hold her voice steady.

A glimmer lightened her brother's face, and Angela breathed a little sigh of thanksgiving. Thomas looked pleased—not upset.

"And you have given an answer?" prompted Thomas.

Angela could not speak. She simply nodded her head, but there was a gleam in her own eyes now.

"I take it from the shine in your eyes that the answer was yes," said Thomas.

Angela nodded again, a smile blossoming on her full mouth, her cheeks flushing faintly.

"When?" asked Thomas simply.

"No date has been set," responded Angela. "We really have not had much chance to make plans at all."

"I know," nodded Thomas. "He's been terribly busy."

"And it wouldn't seem right to—to hurry into marriage with circumstances as they are, and all."

Thomas looked a bit puzzled. "Circumstances?"

"With his father just being buried and—"

Thomas jerked upright, his whole body tensing. His eyes looked startled and unbelieving in the dim light of the lamp.

"What are you talking about?" he demanded.

"Carter wouldn't want to marry quickly. His father—"

"I know about his father."

Angela understood then. Thomas had not been thinking of Carter Stratton when she had announced that she was to marry. Thomas had thought she was speaking of someone else. But who? Who other than Carter would Thomas have assumed to be the one? Who had already been given Thomas's blessing? And why were his eyes now filled with concern?

"I—I don't understand—" began Angela.

Thomas had dropped his head and was running a nervous hand through his thatch of blond hair. At last he looked up, his eyes dark with anxiety.

"It's not that—I mean—" He hesitated and took a deep breath. "Are you sure? I mean, do you really—?"

"Of course," said Angela with more confidence than she felt. After all, wasn't her marriage to Carter going to solve problems for all of them?

Thomas looked at her for a long moment.

"Then you have my blessing," he finally said, but to Angela, his voice sounded weary.

She reached out to squeeze his hand, flashing him a smile so that she might receive one of his in return.

He managed the smile. And he responded to the pressure of her hand. But Angela wondered if both were forced.

"I—I wonder," he finally managed, "if it would be wise to just—just keep your secret—for a—a while—until—until we get this matter of the land settlement behind us."

Angela nodded. She had forgotten about the will. Although she wasn't sure she understood exactly what Thomas was saying, she was content to abide by his wishes.

Chapter Nineteen

Carter

It was difficult for Angela to keep her secret from Mrs. Andrews on Christmas Day. But each time she was tempted to bring up her engagement, she remembered Thomas's request and fought back the urge. She didn't let herself think about the fact that Thane seemed to be avoiding any eye contact with her. She had enough on her mind already.

At the end of the day, the family bundled up with robes and blankets and started off for home. They were filled with turkey and trimmings and new memories of fun and laughter with their good friends.

But as Angela reflected on the day, she felt a stab of pain. This would likely be the last Christmas spent with the Andrews family. Surely Carter would expect to celebrate Christmas in their own home in the future.

Angela brushed away tears that started to spill. She loved the Andrewses. They were like family.

January turned bitterly cold. Angela hated to send the youngsters off to school. A few mornings she did keep them at home, putting them to work on their lessons at the kitchen table.

Carter had not been to call. Angela kept telling herself that it was much too cold for anyone to be out, but she did wonder about his absence.

The trial date was drawing closer. Angela could hardly bear the suspense. She was tempted to bundle up and head for the nearby farm. Surely Gus would be able to give her some news. Perhaps she would even be lucky enough to visit at the same time Charlie was making one of his calls.

But what would she do if Carter should be there? So Angela did not head across the field. She knew Thomas would oppose her going out in such weather. She stayed put, trying to ignore her troubled thoughts, and waited.

Thane dropped in a couple of times in spite of the weather.

"I hear you've been missing me," he said to Sara with a wink. "Or is it just the lemon drops?"

Sara denied the charge with a shake of her blond pigtails, but she did smile brightly when Thane produced her favorite candy.

Thane and Thomas set up the checker board by the cozy kitchen fire and spent the next hour noisily challenging each other. Angela felt a strange comfort in the familiar banter that accompanied the game. She had to admit that she had been missing Thane's visits, too.

By the trial date, the weather had eased some. Angela dressed the children in extra layers and sent them off to school. She fought the urge to hitch the team and head for town. From the reports she had received, the trial was to be held in the town hall. But this word had not come to her from Carter. He had not mentioned the hearing, nor had he called since his pre-Christmas proposal of marriage. Angela began to wonder if she had dreamed it, after all.

Thomas must have noticed her agitation but he made no comment.

"I think I'll go on into town," Thomas announced at the dinner table one evening. "Do you care to come along?"

Angela paled. "I don't think so," she answered slowly.

So Angela watched him go, feeling that whatever word he brought back would somehow affect her.

If Carter only had brought it up, Angela kept saying to herself, *I might have been able to explain to him how important the little place is to Charlie.*

At other moments Angela tried to see Carter's point of view and found herself feeling put out with Charlie. *He could have taken his money and gotten a nice little place in town,* she protested during her inner debates. *He didn't have to take Carter's land.*

But no matter which way Angela argued, she could not find peace of mind.

When Thomas returned from town, he told her the matter still had not been settled. Angela felt more agitated than ever.

Thomas did, however, bring with him a note from Carter.

"My darling Angela," he wrote in bold, firm script. "The days have been unbearably long since I last saw you. I cannot wait until this ordeal is over and I will be free to call again and we can make our plans. It shouldn't be long now. Things went well today—in my favor, I might add, and I propose that soon I will be granted the land that is rightfully mine. This fool of a little man really doesn't have a logical argument on his side. So please bear with me. I will call the moment I am free to do so. With my deepest affection, Carter."

Angela was relieved to hear from him but troubled at his assessment of Charlie.

He's not a fool of a little man, she argued to herself. *He is a dear, good friend and he does have right to the land. It was left to him.*

But Angela would not have shared her thoughts or her words with anyone. Not even Thomas. To do so would have been to put some blame on Carter.

"It will all be over soon," she said out loud, pretending to find comfort in that fact.

Angela hoped that Carter would call, but two days passed and still he had not visited.

"That trial must be dragging on and on," she fumed in exasperation. Thomas nodded and went back to the farm account numbers on his sheet of paper.

It was Charlie who eventually brought the news.

When she heard the knock Angela jumped to her feet, brushing first at her hair and then at her skirt, sure that Carter was on the other side of the door. But when Thomas opened it, it was Charlie who stood there, a grin on his face.

"It's over?" asked Thomas.

Charlie grinned wider.

"Come in," welcomed Thomas.

Charlie moved into the kitchen, pulling his worn hat from his head as he did so. He beat the hat against his leg a couple of times to shake the loose snow from its brim, then tossed it toward the corner and moved to the warmth of the fire.

Angela held her breath. She couldn't have said a word if the kitchen had been on fire.

"How did it go?" asked Thomas, though Angela felt that he already knew.

"I licked 'im," boasted Charlie. "Licked 'im fair and square."

Angela had never heard Charlie gloat in such a fashion before. For a moment she felt sick to her stomach.

"So you got your land?"

"They said the will stood—the way it was written."

Thomas nodded, looking from Charlie to Angela. He wasn't sure how to respond.

"That's good," said Thomas.

Angela said nothing.

"Yeah," said Charlie, slapping his thigh with a heavy mitten. "Yeah."

Then Charlie turned the conversation abruptly. "You busy tomorra?"

"No," said Thomas.

"Wondered iffen you'd bring thet big team of yours and help me move my shack. I figured as how, iffen I could get about four big teams, I could skid it right on over here."

"You're going to move it?"

Charlie turned to Angela. "Remember how you once said to me thet I'd be welcome to live here?"

Angela nodded. She had said that—but things were so different then. What would Carter think about her harboring the enemy? Angela was sure Carter would consider Charlie the enemy now.

"Well, I thought as how I'd like to have thet shack right

up there in the corner by the garden—iffen the offer still stands, thet is?"

Angela felt that it was hardly the time to tell Charlie they themselves might not be living on the farm for long. When she married, the children would go with her, and Thomas would go off to do his research work. She opened her mouth to speak, but Thomas shook his head. She closed her mouth quickly and turned to the stove.

"I don't understand," said Thomas slowly. "Of course you're welcome here. But you don't want your shack on your own land by the creek?"

Charlie began to chuckle as if he had just played a delightful joke on someone.

"Don't have any land by the crick," he informed them.

"But I thought you said you won."

"I did. I did," said Charlie with shining eyes. "They gave me the land—then I took the deed—and I looked young Mr. Stratton straight in the eye an told 'im thet I'd move my shack and he could have his land fer all I cared—an' I handed thet deed right back to 'im."

"But—but if you didn't care about the land, why did you go to court?" asked Thomas incredulously.

Charlie's eyes began to snap. "I weren't gonna be pushed around by some young city-slicker," he sputtered. "The land was mine. Fair and square. It was given to me by the *owner*. The *inheritor* doesn't have no say so in the matter. He needn't think thet he can jest walk in and stomp all over folks."

"But court cases cost—"

"Didn't cost me," said Charlie, his eyes twinkling again. "Cost 'im. He had to pay the court costs." Charlie continued chuckling. "An' he got hisself laughed at, too. The whole court room was laughing. Here he spent all thet money, I won the case, and then I give it back to 'im. Iffen he'd asked face-to-face like a man in the first place, I'd a give it to 'im to begin with, but bein' ordered around by a bunch of papers don't sit well with me."

Poor Carter, Angela thought. *No wonder he hasn't come around.*

Then Angela felt anger toward both men begin to seep through her. Carter was wrong to try to muscle his way with Charlie. But Charlie was equally improper to let the whole mess get to court just to prove his silly point. In Angela's thinking they had both acted like spoiled children. She turned her back and headed for the stairway.

She stopped mid-stride, realizing she was being just as foolish herself. *Never return evil for evil,* she heard the words clearly in her memory. Her mama would have been ashamed of the way she was acting.

It took a moment of silent prayer for her to regain her composure, but at last she was able to turn and speak evenly.

"Cup of coffee, Charlie?" she asked and even managed a small smile.

It was almost the end of January before Carter finally got around to calling. Angela had begun to think she would never see him again. But when he came he was just as solicitous as ever, as though he had not been absent for an entire month. He seemed to take up right where he had left off, offering no explanation or apology for his long absence.

"I hear the trial is finally over," Angela eventually said.

"Yes," he nodded, seeming pleased with himself. "I have all my land back in one piece."

Angela wondered if he had noticed the small shack tucked away by the back garden. If so, he made no comment.

"I am leaving soon for Atlanta again," he informed her. "I have workmen coming to start on the house, but there are a few more things I need to finalize."

He beamed at Angela, and she knew he expected her to be happy at the news. She simply nodded her head in acknowledgment.

He took her hand. "What special thing might I bring you, my dear, as an engagement gift?" he asked.

Angela was taken by surprise. She had not thought of an engagement gift and had no idea what would be appropriate.

161

"I—I don't know," she stammered. "Perhaps you should do the choosing."

Her answer apparently satisfied him. He nodded as though it made the best of sense.

"How long will you be gone?" she asked.

"I have no way of knowing. I do hope it won't take too long. I can't bear to be away from you. Perhaps I can arrange for us to take a trip together later on. There are so many things I want to show you. There is so much shopping for you to do for your trousseau. There is so much for you to learn about the proper running of a house." He flushed slightly and then hurried on, "Of course, I know you have kept house for years. But now you will have help with the work—it will be the supervision you will need to learn."

Angela couldn't imagine herself supervising rather than doing the work herself.

"We have so many things we need to talk about," he went on.

"Yes," agreed Angela. "We do."

"Would you like me to look for an extra housekeeper while I am there?"

"An extra housekeeper?"

"For here. For the children."

"Oh, but the children won't be staying here," Angela quickly said, wondering why it was necessary to explain this to Carter.

"You have some place else for them?"

"Why, they'll be with me," replied Angela.

"But my dear," responded Carter with one of his measured smiles, "I plan to take you to live with me."

Angela nodded. "Of course."

Carter seemed to catch on at last. "You mean," he said slowly, "that you propose to bring all of them along with you to my house?"

Angela nodded, her stomach beginning to churn. By the look on his face she realized he really had meant to leave the youngsters here on their own.

He shook his head slowly and then his eyes began to twinkle. "How you tease," he laughed, giving her a playful shake.

"Carter," said Angela, her back straightening, "I am not one to tease about such serious matters."

She looked directly into his eyes and saw her own image reflected in them, a bit of a girl with honey blond hair. Her blue eyes held his steadily, and her small frame did not flinch. Carter shifted his weight to his other foot.

"You can't be serious!" he finally exclaimed.

"They go—or I stay," stated Angela simply. "I haven't been much of a mother—but I am the only mother they have. I will not leave them until they have been properly raised."

Carter shifted again. "I can't believe you," he said at last, his eyes narrowing. Then he smiled, but not his sweet, charming smile. "I'm afraid, my dear, that you are all set to be an old maid. No man will marry a woman who brings along three younger siblings—even if she is pleasing to the eye."

Angela swallowed hard and nodded. "Then so be it," she replied with all the courage she could muster. She moved to get his hat and coat and handed them to him without a word.

He looked at her, anger filling his eyes, and then he began to laugh, a coarse, bitter laugh that made Angela shiver. She felt as though she had been struck, but still she did not flinch.

"Good night, my dear," he said.

"Goodbye, Mr. Stratton," she replied and turned back to the fire until she heard him leave the room.

It wasn't until Angela was in the privacy of her own bedroom that she allowed the tears to flow. She didn't bother to remove her clothes before throwing herself onto her bed and letting the sobs shake her slender body.

"He's right," she cried into her pillow. "He's right. I will be an old maid. No one will ever, ever marry me with three others to care for. I know it. I know it."

Angela cried long and hard, but in the end she wiped her tears and resolutely got up to prepare for bed.

"I don't care," she told her image in the mirror. "I am quite ready to be an old maid. I made Mama a promise—and with God's help I will keep it. I will raise them. I will. I will. And I will never—never look at another man again. How could I have been so foolish? Why did I say yes so quickly? Mama taught me more sense than that. Thomas was right. I never really knew Carter. I did not realize the kind of person he really is. I am just so thankful—so thankful—that I found out in time to prevent—to prevent a—a tragic mistake."

She lifted her chin and straightened her back in resolve—but she couldn't keep another tear from trickling down her cheek.

Chapter Twenty

Changing Plans

Charlie came in for coffee the next morning.

Angela sensed something was bothering him, but he made no comment. Instead, he talked with Thomas about the latest storm, wondered how Gus was getting along with his new boss, and promised Angela that come spring, he would help her with her garden.

"Is your cabin warm enough?" Thomas asked.

Charlie nodded, pride in his eyes.

"I helped the boss build thet little place. We made sure thet it was sound and solid," he said, the gleam in his eyes again. "Got everything in there thet a man needs."

So why aren't you happy? Angela wanted to ask, but she held her tongue.

Thomas asked the question Angela was thinking, though in a roundabout way. He simply gave Charlie the opportunity to bring up what was bothering him. "What can we do for you, Charlie?"

Charlie sat and stirred the cream in his coffee. Round and round went his spoon, and Angela imagined his thoughts going round and round, too. It was a long time before he spoke.

"Been doin' some thinkin'," Charlie said at last. "It really weren't right the way I handled young Mr. Stratton. I mean— well, he is the boss's boy—an' I reckon iffen it had been me— I woulda wanted all of my pa's land myself. I coulda jest given him back his land—not made a public show of it like I did."

There was silence again. Charlie raised his head, his eyes troubled.

"Reckon yer pa would've done it different," he said with conviction.

Thomas nodded. "Reckon," he agreed.

"Well, I been thinkin' as to how I owe the young feller an apology," said Charlie.

Angela stiffened. At one point she would have agreed, but after the events of the previous evening she had little compassion for Carter Stratton.

"Well, I figure as how I best hike myself on over there and speak my little piece. Don't know if he'll accept my words or not—but I gotta be a sayin' 'em—iffen I want to live with myself, that is."

Thomas nodded.

They sat in silence again. Angela wished to speak—wished to stir—wished to flee—but she did none of those things. Her own thoughts went round and round in her head.

"I watched yer folks fer a good number of years," Charlie went on slowly. "I don't think they would have taken things on—jest fer spite, like I done. Now, mind you—I don't claim to be religious like yer folks were—but they was good folks. Funny—" Charlie hesitated and then chuckled softly, "I find myself thinkin' about yer pa and askin' myself, 'What would Karl have done?' An' yer ma. Well, she was kindness itself. Never done a thing in her life fer spite, yer ma. One time she says to me, 'Charlie, the Lord says we are to forgive seventy times seven,' she says. 'I figure as how I never get much past ten.' She says thet to me, and she smiles an' I think within myself thet I never get much past two. Fact is, I most often never even get started."

Angela felt her face warming. She was harboring a little resentment of her own. Charlie was right. Her mama would want her to forgive—if indeed she had any reason to be angry at all. Other suitors had changed their minds about the person they had asked to marry. Certainly Carter had a right to a wife without—without a whole family to tend.

Angela went for more coffee. She would spend some time

with the Lord in prayer just as soon as Charlie left on his little errand.

"Thomas . . ." Angela spoke slowly, hesitantly. She wasn't sure just where or how to start. She could feel tears forming and willed herself not to cry like a silly child.

Thomas lifted his head and waited.

Angela turned her attention back to her dinner plate. She had determined that Thomas would be told of the change of plans before the children arrived home from school.

Angela lifted her head, took a deep breath and said, "There won't be a wedding, after all." Her voice was matter-of-fact and straightforward.

Her brother's eyes clouded. Angela read anger in them, and Thomas seldom got angry.

"He backed out?" he said through clenched teeth.

"Let's just say we changed our minds," Angela hurried on. "There were some things we had not discussed—before. And when we got to them, we couldn't work out a compromise," she said simply.

The eyes before her remained dark. Angela hurried on.

"I—I'm sorry," she whispered. "I know that it means— means—" but she could not go on.

The darkness began to fade from her brother's eyes. Thomas gave a little sigh. Was it one of relief? Angela wondered. He reached for her hand and gave it a squeeze. "Are you terribly disappointed?" he asked.

Angela shook her head, tears coming now. "I—I honestly don't know," she managed to say. "In some ways—yes—I—I guess any girl is disappointed when—when things don't work out—as planned." Angela stopped to sniff and wipe at the tears with her handkerchief. "But I—I've done some praying and I think—I think that—well, I think it's best this way. I don't think Carter and I—that we were—well—right for each other. But I'm awfully sorry about you. I mean—"

"About me?" cut in Thomas. "What do you mean 'about me'?"

"Well, you could have left the farm. Gone to do your work with seed like you've always dreamed—"

Thomas stood. "You mean you thought—"

"I know how much it means to you," she rushed on, "and as long as you need to be here—for the children and me—I know you won't just leave us and go," said Angela with a little shrug.

Thomas sat down again and leaned toward his sister. "Angela," he said softly but firmly, "don't you ever marry anyone—*anyone,* you hear?—to try to make things better for the rest of the family."

"But it wasn't—wasn't just that," Angela fumbled. "I mean—I mean I—I liked Carter. He was—was—"

"Arrogant, conceited, and totally uncaring of another's feelings," Thomas said, his voice hard.

It was Angela's turn to stand to her feet. Her eyes were wide with shock and her lower lip trembled in spite of her attempts to still it with her teeth.

"You thought that?"

Thomas was already repentant. He lowered his head and ran his hand through his hair. "I'm sorry. I'm sorry," he muttered.

"Thomas," said Angela reaching out a hand to her brother. "Why? Why didn't you say so?"

For a moment Thomas could not respond, but at last he looked directly at Angela. "Because I thought you loved him."

Angela dropped to her chair again. "So did I," she whispered. "For a short time—so did I."

"And now?" asked Thomas.

"I spent a good part of the morning in prayer. Oh, Thomas. I don't think it would have been right at all. Mama would have—Mama would have known right from the start. I know she would have. I could have been saved the heartbreak if only Mama—"

"Don't," said Thomas. "Don't berate yourself. You got it worked out. That's all that matters now. We'll just—we'll just go on as though it never happened."

Angela shook her head. She knew she would always be

aware of the fact that she had been engaged—then jilted. But she lifted her chin and looked at Thomas. Then her eyes began to twinkle and her lips formed a wobbly smile.

"I'll live," she said. "I've been wooed and—and forsaken— but the worst is already over. Life will go on." She blinked back an insistent tear.

Thomas stood and pulled her into his arms. For a moment Angela leaned against his broad chest, comforted by the strength of the arms that held her. She would have missed Thomas. But she was so sorry—so sorry that he couldn't pursue his dream.

"Good girl," Thomas said.

His voice sounded so much like their father's that Angela felt like a little girl again, held safe in her pa's strong arms.

"Good girl," Thomas said again; then he released her and went for his cap and heavy coat.

———

Life did go on for Angela. Nothing further was said about the broken engagement. Angela was thankful that Thomas wisely had asked her not to tell anyone of her wedding plans. There were no questions from friends and neighbors to answer. But in her heart, Angela still felt moments of pain.

Fortunately there were few occasions for her to see Carter. Word had it that he was much too busy on the ranch to make it to Sunday church. He did manage the Easter Sunday service, but he sat near the back and Angela did not have to greet him. Occasionally they met on the streets of the little town and Angela managed a stiff smile and a "good morning." Carter responded in a manner to indicate that Angela had never been anyone special in his life. Angela heard that he was calling at the home of Trudie Sommers, but she did not make any effort to verify or discredit those rumors.

Winter turned to spring and Charlie kept good his word about helping Angela plant her garden. She was surprised how much time it freed when Charlie manned the hoe.

Thomas planted a large plot of his special seed even before he did the regular planting. He could hardly wait for the new grain to appear so he could judge its success.

School ended and the children were home again. Angela always looked forward to that time of year. It wasn't hard to keep them busy as there were many jobs around the farmhouse. Derek spent his time helping Thomas in the fields. He was filling out, and even though Angela still thought of him as a young boy, she knew he was quickly becoming a young man.

His attitude about himself and about life seemed to improve—but very slowly. Angela knew the pain in his past would likely always haunt him. They still played the memory game, and Derek shared along with the rest. Some stories were poignant, some funny, others joyous. Angela hoped their game helped healing to occur.

Louise had far more interest in socializing than in fulfilling household chores. She begged and pestered until Angela was tempted to tell her to just be gone and leave the household in peace. But Angela knew her mother would not have handled it in that manner.

"You may have one outing a week," she told her young sister. "You must decide whether it is to be an evening, an afternoon, or a Sunday."

Louise sulked for a time but at last accepted the arrangement.

Sara had grown so much over the winter months that Angela had to let down every inch of her sister's skirts. She would soon be passing on to Louise's hand-me-down dresses. Angela sensed that Sara would be the tall one—tall and slim like their father. But the growth of the young girl made Angela uneasy. Did it mean that she was about to lose the joyful, teasing, carefree little bundle of energy called Sara and gain another changing, pouting, testing adolescent? Angela wasn't sure she would be able to cope with two moody teenagers.

Thane was back. He spent every available minute in the fields with Thomas and Derek. He challenged Thomas to checker games and teased Louise about young men of the community. He brought Sara her lemon drops and licorice sticks and helped Derek fashion a bridle for his new saddle horse.

He brought groceries from the store for Charlie and recommended medication for his arthritis. He lounged on the front veranda, talking and laughing, while the long hours of dusk wrapped a soft, dark cloak about the farm. He admired Angela's garden, asked for her company on summer evening walks, brought her books from his own bookshelves, and listened to her plans for sewing new curtains.

And it was true. He did watch her carefully—just like Sara had said. But Angela hardly noticed. She felt at ease with Thane. He was as close as one of the family. There was a security—a fellowship—a feeling of belonging. Angela sensed it, though she could not have defined it. But she, like the others, was very glad that Thane was back.

Chapter Twenty-one

The Picnic

The day was warm with just the hint of a breeze. Angela spent the morning in her kitchen preparing potato salad and deviled eggs. From the oven the chicken sent out the most inviting aroma. Angela had browned it in the big frying pan, then covered it with herbs and rich cream and put it into the oven to simmer. Louise cut thick slices of homemade bread, and Sara spread them generously with farm butter, making sure that even the corners and crusts were given a portion.

"Thomas hates dry edges," she observed as she worked.

Louise looked at the cake on the table. It was her first baking for the community picnic and she appeared proud of her work. With a toss of her pinned-up hair, she went back to slicing the bread.

"What time is dinner?" she asked.

Angela answered without looking up from her task. "One o'clock."

Louise glanced toward the mantel clock. "I hope the boys hurry or we'll be late."

Angela looked at the clock as well. "There's lots of time," she assured the younger girl.

"Does Trudie still like Thomas?" asked Sara without any preamble.

Angela shifted her gaze to Sara. Her dress, even though let down to the limit, was still a bit too short. She sighed. How would she ever keep up with the growing child?

173

"I—I hear that"—Angela almost said Carter, then changed it quickly to Mr. Stratton—"that Mr. Stratton has been calling on Trudie."

"Good!" said Sara with emphasis but made no explanation.

The back door slammed and Derek entered the kitchen, his eyes shining. "Ready?" he called in an excited tone.

Angela felt her pulse quicken. It was the first time she had seen the boy so enthusiastic.

"We just need to bundle things up," she told him. "Bring those boxes from the shed and we'll wrap the chicken so it won't cool."

Derek hastened to obey, and Angela began to gather the picnic foods for packing. With the help of the girls, she soon had things ready to go, and Thomas and Derek carried the boxes to the waiting wagon. Charlie was already standing by, looking pleased.

"Been ages since I found myself at a picnic," he observed. "And with a real live family too," he added, smiling around on them all.

Angela noticed that he looked pleased at the prospect.

They all climbed aboard and found places to sit; then Thomas clucked to the team and they were off.

Angela lifted her eyes to the cloudless sky. "Well, it looks like we won't be rained out," she observed. "Though it could get a mite hot before the day is over."

"Just right," said Derek, slapping a well-worn baseball into the mitt on his hand.

Angela knew why Derek was excited about the day. He loved sports, and he lost no opportunity to take part in a game.

"Well, if you want to play ball," Thomas counseled good-naturedly, "remember not to eat too much. Hard to play ball on a full stomach."

"Why don't we play ball first?" asked Derek.

"Because the food wouldn't stay hot—or cold—whatever it is supposed to be," explained Angela.

"Still think they have it backwards," mused Derek, showing little concern as to whether hot dishes became cool or cold dishes became warm.

"You'd get sick," said Louise with a familiar toss of her head. "Food spoils real fast in the summer heat."

The occupants of the wagon fell silent then, each sorting out personal thoughts. Angela wondered if she would need to face Carter and Trudie as a twosome. The thought didn't bother her as much as it would have a few months previously, but still it would be a less-than-pleasant experience. She marveled, though, that she had returned to emotional health so quickly.

A number of teams had already gathered by the time Thomas hitched his team to the rail fence. Sara had jumped out to join her friends before the wagon even rolled to a stop. Angela was about to call after her to walk like a lady, but she shook her head and turned back to the dinner items.

Long tables had been constructed for the food, and Angela directed Thomas and Derek to carry the pans and boxes. Charlie lent a hand and soon the task was complete and Derek was free to find other young men with whom to discuss the ball game. Thomas drifted to where young fellows his own age had gathered. Louise tossed her head slightly and displayed her cake, obviously wishing someone would ask her who had made it.

The meal was first on the agenda. Long lines of chattering, laughing neighbors queued up, and impatient children crowded to the front of the line to get "first pick." Angela found herself in line beside Thane.

"Sara tells me that Louise baked a cake," he whispered in her ear. "Which one is it so I can make an announcement?"

Angela laughed as she pointed out Louise's cake. Thane nodded, and Angela was sure then that Louise would receive all of the recognition she desired.

Sure enough, when they reached the spot, Thane declared in a loud voice, "Look at that cake! It looks delicious. I wonder who made it. Do you know?" he asked Mrs. Blackwell, who was on the other side of the table.

She shook her head.

"Do you know?" he asked Mrs. Sommers.

She gave the same response.

"It looks delicious," he repeated and went on helping himself to a generous portion. "Must be a good cook. Louise, do you know?" he called to her just ahead of them in the line.

Louise's face reddened, but she admitted ownership. "I did," she said with a self-conscious tilt of her blond head.

"By yourself?" asked Thane in astounded tones.

Louise nodded. Angela could see the pleased look in her sister's eyes as heads turned to look.

Thane, who had already dipped his fork into the piece on his plate as though he couldn't wait another second, was smacking his lips. "Yum. It tastes even better than it looks. Delicious!"

Angela chuckled. If Louise wanted recognition, word had certainly gotten to the right person. Angela was about to give Thane a nudge to caution him not to go too far. But Thane suddenly turned the compliment toward her, making Angela blush as red as Louise.

"Well, she should be good," he whispered into her ear; "she's had the community's best teacher."

Angela was eager to quiet Thane's embarrassing comments, so she led him to the shade of tall poplar trees that bordered the school property. The Andrews family joined them, and their talk turned to a more comfortable topic than cakes and cooks.

After dinner the games and races began. Thomas took part in everything for which he was eligible. Sometimes he won, sometimes he lost, but he accepted both outcomes with good humor. He took first place in the woodcutting competition with no difficulty, retaining his title for the third year.

Derek proved to be good at foot racing. But Derek entered only those events in which he felt he would make a fair show. *Derek does not do very well at losing,* Angela observed, noticing the intensity of his face.

Louise scorned involvement in competition. She tossed her head, trying to look mature, but she wasn't always able to quite manage it. Sara, on the other hand, had no inhibitions and would have raced with the boys had it been allowed.

From one event to another the day progressed with everyone having a lot of fun. Then it was time for the ball game, and the Merrifield brothers were called on to choose up sides. Spectators moved their blankets to grassy spots near the diamond, and folks settled themselves for some cheering. Roger Merrifield chose Derek to be on his team, and his brother Peter chose Thomas.

"Brother against brother," Angela heard someone say, and the comment was followed by a laugh.

About the time of the first pitch Angela saw Carter's team of bays enter the schoolyard. By his side sat Trudie, proudly holding his arm with one hand and her hat with the other. The team came to a halt in a small cloud of dust, and Trudie descended like a queen. She leaned close to Carter as they walked toward the crowd and laughed noisily as he spread their blanket. Angela turned her eyes back to the game. It did bother her—a little.

The game held her attention, though. The score remained even inning by inning. Derek's team was ahead by a run—then Thomas's team would lead—back and forth, back and forth. Angela hardly knew how to cheer, so she cheered for both.

When they went into the ninth inning the score was tied. Thomas's team batted first. Peter struck out. Ernest hit the ball down the first base line, and Thane disposed of that batter. The third batter hit a long fly ball. Angela held her breath. It was heading straight toward Derek. No, it was going to his right. There was no one else who would be able to reach the ball. Derek raced toward it, and Angela squirmed and grimaced. She was sure he had no hope of getting to the fly ball and would be injured in the attempt. At the last possible second, Derek made a valiant dive, rolling head over heels in the grass. When he stopped tumbling he jumped to his feet to show that he had the ball in his gloved hand. The crowd cheered, and Angela started breathing again when she saw the grinning boy running in from left field.

The score was still tied. Angela felt this would be a good time to end the game. No winners or losers. Then she noticed the look on Derek's face. It was clear to Angela that his thinking did not match her own. Derek wanted to win. She watched as he swung the bat in preparation for his turn at the plate. On his face was a look of determination she had never seen before.

Thane was the first batter. He hit the ball well, but Peter managed to catch it. Angela did not know the young man who batted in second place. His family was new to the community. He popped up a foul that was caught by the catcher. There was just one more chance for a win, and Derek stepped to the plate. Angela felt her stomach tighten. She didn't want to watch, but she couldn't bear to turn away.

To make matters worse, the pitcher was Thomas. Everyone talked about what a good pitcher he was. Angela knew little about baseball, but she was willing to take the word of the neighborhood young men. If they said Thomas was good, she concluded he must be.

Brother faced brother. Thomas stood on the mound, his face relaxed, his eyes showing both humor at the situation and pride in his younger brother. Derek stared back, his jaw tight, his eyes intense, his whole frame flexed for action. He had faced Thomas many times before. They often filled vacant moments with a ball and bat in the farmyard. But Thomas had always thrown balls he wanted his brother to hit. This time, Derek knew, there would be no mercy.

Derek whipped the bat in little flicking motions that Angela likened to the tail of a hunting cat. Thomas's moves were slow, deliberate. He took his sign from the catcher, started his windup, then reared back and threw a sizzling fast ball. Derek swung—but too late.

"Strike one," called Mr. Andrews from behind his umpire's mask.

Derek shuffled, digging in his forward foot with determination.

Thomas looked at the catcher and ground the ball in his mitt.

Angela's stomach was twisting now. Men had risen from their blankets, their eyes squinting against the afternoon sun. An occasional yell rent the stillness, but most leaned forward in silence, ready to explode should the drama intensify.

Thomas threw two balls in succession. "Just nicked the plate," Angela heard the man to her left exclaim. "Andrews missed that call."

But the count stood—two and one.

Another pitch came spinning in. Angela wondered how Derek could even see it, but he swung, sending the ball reeling into the dirt at his feet.

Two and two.

The next pitch was in close. For one horrible moment Angela feared it would strike Derek, but it veered away and Derek jumped back, avoiding any contact.

Three and two. Full count. The crowd leaned into the play. Even Carter had deserted Trudie to stand with the others, his jaw working, his eyes intense.

Angela's eyes shifted quickly back to her two brothers. The one on the mound, rubbing the ball in his glove, and the other at the plate, sweat beading on his forehead, his bat flicking, his muscles taut.

Another pitch. Angela could not look. She closed her eyes just as the ball was about to reach the plate. Then she heard a sharp, loud crack.

She jerked her head up again and was on her feet before she realized what she was doing. "Run, run!" she screamed as Derek headed for first base. The ball was still in the air. It was sailing farther and farther. Angela saw Thomas, his back to home plate. He was shading his eyes and watching the flight of the ball.

When Angela's eyes returned to Derek she was surprised to see him rounding second—then on to third. The ball had gone over the heads of the outfielders and was being chased by the centerfielder. The throw was coming in as Derek tagged third, but he kept running full speed toward home base.

"Slide! Slide!" Angela heard someone yell, and she thought the voice sounded like Thomas's.

Derek dove head first beneath the catcher. The ball smacked into the glove just as Derek's hand stretched forward to touch the plate. He had averted the tag. A cheer went up.

The crowd surged forward as one. Derek's team had won the game.

Angela felt tears stinging her eyes. She knew how much the win would mean to her little brother. She had no fear that the loss would adversely affect Thomas.

She fought her way back to her blanket against the pushing crowd, her face flushed at her lack of composure.

A strange silence settled about her. She turned back to the diamond, bewildered. Something was wrong. Had Mr. Andrews called Derek out? But he was safe. He had slid.

And then, through the gathering crowd, Angela saw the reason for the stillness. Derek was still on the ground. He had not picked himself up from the dirt. He lay—just where he had fallen. Thomas was bending over him, speaking his name, brushing his cheek. Angela saw fear in his eyes. Derek lay still. Very still.

With a cry Angela grabbed up her skirts and ran toward them. She tried to pray but the only words to come from her lips were "Oh, God. Oh, God."

"Bring some water," someone was saying.

"He must have hit his head," said another.

Angela fell on her knees beside Thomas and reached out a hand to Derek.

"Don't move him," cautioned Thomas, brushing her hand aside.

Angela looked up at him, her eyes filled with terror. "Is he—?"

"I don't know. I don't know," said Thomas. "But we can't move him until we're sure he hasn't hurt his neck or something."

Angela nodded, tears spilling down her face. *Oh, God, if anything happens to Derek*—She couldn't finish the thought.

He was so still. So pale. Angela reached a hand to his cheek and gently brushed off a smudge of dust.

"They've run for Doc," someone said, and someone else knelt beside her and wiped Derek's face with a water-soaked towel.

A moan escaped Derek's lips. It was the most beautiful

sound Angela had ever heard. Then he stirred slightly.

"Don't move," cautioned Thomas, holding the boy steady. "It's all right, Derek. It's all right. Just lie still. Lie still."

Derek moaned again.

The doctor came from his shaded spot on the other side of the schoolyard, and the crowd receded while he knelt beside the young boy. Angela frantically watched his probing fingers as they felt Derek's neck, shoulders, chest.

"Just winded," he said at last. "He got the breath knocked right out of him."

Derek's eyes fluttered open and he looked up, bewildered, then embarrassed by all the attention.

"Just lie still a minute, son," the doctor said. "Just lie still. Here, Thomas—help me turn him onto his back."

An older man placed his hat on the ground for a pillow, while the Doc and Thomas turned Derek. Doc took over sponging the boy's face, and Angela saw the color gradually return. The crowd started to breathe again.

"That's better," said Doc. "That's better." Then with a twinkle in his eye he said to Derek, "Hear you won the game."

Derek grinned and the whole group erupted into a cheer. The tension broke. Derek was going to be fine.

Angela felt her knees buckle beneath her. She had never fainted before, but she knew she was going down now. But someone caught her and helped her to the blanket she had earlier deserted. She heard a voice ask for a cup of water. She felt her head cradled against a shoulder, and she left it there until her world stopped spinning. She accepted the water offered to her and soon her equilibrium began to return.

"I'm fine," she finally muttered, embarrassed at her near collapse.

"You're sure?"

She nodded her head emphatically and looked up into the face of Thane.

"I'm fine," she said again. "It just sort of—sort of gave me a scare."

Thane nodded. Then his eyes began to twinkle. "He won," he whispered. "He won. He beat Tom's best pitch. You should see Thomas. Now that he's over his fright—he's fairly bursting his buttons."

Chapter Twenty-two

Visitors

Angela had just finished the morning laundry and Louise was hanging the last of the socks on the clothesline when Mrs. Blackwell arrived, panting from the effort of her walk. Angela ushered the woman into the coolness of the kitchen, fearing that she might suffer from heat exhaustion if she didn't soon get in out of the summer sun.

Angela pushed forward a chair and urged the woman to be seated. Mrs. Blackwell dropped into the chair with a glance toward the icebox.

"Would you like some lemonade?" asked Angela.

The woman nodded, and Angela hastened to produce a large glassful.

After a lengthy drink, Mrs. Blackwell placed the glass on the table but did not release it.

"I hear there's to be a weddin'," she announced.

Angela raised her eyebrows.

"Thet there Stratton fella is hitchin' hisself to Trudie," continued Mrs. Blackwell.

"Really? I hadn't heard," responded Angela. She kept her voice even.

"My man heard the news in town this mornin'. Says it's to be soon—in the church. 'Course her folks wouldn't be none too happy iffen she didn't marry in the church."

Angela nodded.

"Well, I don't like the smell of it all," went on the woman.

"Seems awful fast work to me. He ain't been here in the community fer thet long."

Angela wondered what the woman would say if she knew Carter Stratton had already been betrothed to another since his arrival in their community.

Mrs. Blackwell took another long drink.

"Some folks is sayin' thet he's jest out to spite his ma. He and her had 'em a big fight before he left home." She spoke the last statement in a hushed, confidential tone.

When Angela didn't respond, Mrs. Blackwell continued. "His ma wants him to marry a city girl. Even had one all picked out fer him. He's pickin' his own jest to get back at her."

She finished the lemonade and pushed the empty glass toward Angela.

Angela refilled it and passed it back.

"His ma won't even come to the weddin'." She made a disapproving sound at this last bit of information.

Angela wondered how much truth there was to the report. If true, if Carter was marrying just for spite—she herself could have been the unfortunate bride. *But surely, surely he wouldn't do that,* she reasoned. Not to Trudie. Not to anyone. Angela forced the gossip from her mind and attempted to divert the conversation.

"How is your garden doing?"

"See thet man out hoein' yours 'most every time I go by," the woman stated instead of answering the question. "You really think yer ma would have been happy with an old man livin' with ya?"

"He doesn't live with us," corrected Angela. "He lives all alone—in his little cabin."

"Same thing," said the woman with a dark look. "He comes an' goes like he lives here. An' you with two innocent young girls an' all. Yer mama—"

"My mama was a charitable woman," Angela stated flatly. "And she did not look for dirt on a polished table. Charlie needed a place for his cabin—and Thomas appreciates an older, wiser head for farming advice. And as for me and the girls, Charlie is like a—like a grandfather—and we need all the family we can muster."

The woman's mouth dropped at Angela's frankness. Her eyes flashed, but she held her tongue and reached for another drink from the glass.

Angela spun away from her. The idea that anyone would even hint there was anything wrong with Charlie sharing their yard made her tremble with anger.

But she had only taken two steps before she turned again. She stood for a moment in silence and then dipped her head. "I'm sorry," she said softly, lifting her chin again. "My mama would not be proud of my sharp tongue. Charlie is a dear friend of the family and we are—are happy to have him living here. But Mama—Mama would never tolerate sass or disrespect of our elders. For that, I apologize."

The older woman did not decline or accept the apology, and Angela went for some sugar cookies to accompany the lemonade. When she returned, the incident seemed to have been forgotten.

The very next day Trudie came calling. Angela was in the kitchen kneading dough for a batch of bread. Louise worked over the ironing board, and Sara labored over stitching a torn pocket on one of her frocks.

Trudie bustled into the kitchen without waiting to be invited. Her eyes shone and her mass of red hair, carelessly piled on top of her bouncing head, danced in rhythm to her enthusiasm.

"Guess what?" she squealed, holding out her arms to Angela. Angela did not have to guess, but she remained silent.

"Oh, guess what?" Trudie repeated. "I'm going to be married!" She threw herself at Angela with an excited squeal, and Angela returned the embrace even though her heart was not in it. The young woman's face glowed and her eyes shone.

"Oh, look!" Angela exclaimed when they backed away from each other. "I've smeared flour all over your shoulder."

Trudie just laughed as though the flour was part of the exciting world she inhabited. Angela grabbed a towel and tried to brush Trudie's dress, but Trudie just laughed harder.

"Don't fret. Don't fret," she giggled. "Carter is taking me shopping in the city anyway. I'm to have all new clothes. Everything. He said so."

Angela tossed the towel down on the seat of a nearby chair. "In that case," she responded with a laugh, "another hug." Angela was surprised that she could enjoy this moment with her friend. She sincerely hoped Trudie would be happy with Carter.

Trudie accepted the second hug with the same enthusiasm she had given the first, and Angela did not try to keep her floured hands from the shoulders of the blue dress.

"Now sit—and tell me all about it," Angela invited.

"We are getting married in two weeks—on Sunday afternoon in the church. We will have the dinner at the farm. We have a big yard there as you know, so just—just everyone will be able to come. Do pray that it will be a nice day. I'll just die if it rains—or is windy.

"Carter is arranging for flowers—they have flowers in the city for their weddings—and I am wearing a gown right from a city shop. Carter has it already, but he won't let me see it until the wedding morning."

"Well, that is a turn," mused Angela. *I thought the groom was the one who was not to see it.*

"Carter is paying for everything. He has told Mama exactly what he wants for the ceremony and the dinner and everything."

Angela said nothing.

"But he is letting me choose my own attendant," Trudie continued. Then she squealed again and held out her arms to Angela as before. "I picked *you.*"

Angela felt the blood draining from her face. "Oh, but I—"

"No, don't you try to say no. You are my best friend."

"But what will Carter—"

"I've already told Carter. He says he'd love to have you share our happy moment. He was so sweet about it. He will even shop for a dress for you. He insists—he says he'll pick one just made for you."

Angela had to sit down. She was glad to find a chair nearby.

She couldn't guess what Carter would choose for her. An ugly dress that looked frumpish and demeaning—or a stylish gown to remind her of what she could have had. Either way, she was not looking forward to seeing the dress or taking part in this wedding.

Trudie was still babbling. "And he said he would look after everything. And, oh—you should see the house! Carter has had it completely redone. It's gorgeous! And I am to have help—in the kitchen and with the cleaning. Not Gus, of course. Gus has been dismissed. There's a new cook coming from the city. Carter says he is sick and tired of flapjacks and fried bacon." Trudie stopped to laugh as though the comment had been witty or cute.

Poor Gus, thought Angela. *I wonder if Charlie knows. Poor Charlie.*

Trudie went on and on about the wedding, about the house, about Carter. Angela tried to listen but her thoughts kept wandering. Louise had stopped ironing and was listening with wide eyes. Even the young Sara had let her garment fall into her lap and was sitting still, taking in the one-sided conversation.

Angela continued to knead the dough, giving it such a thorough rolling and pounding that she wasn't sure it would have the strength to rise.

At length Trudie slowed down. "Well, I must run," she bubbled. "I have so much to do."

"But I thought Carter was doing it all," responded Louise with youthful frankness.

"Oh, he is—at least all of the big things. He has saved me so much, the dear, but I still have a multitude of little things to attend to. Oh, I'm so glad that you are to be my bridesmaid, Angela. It's going to be such a wonderful day." And with those words Trudie left in a flurry, just as she had arrived.

"Did I say I would be her bridesmaid?" Angela asked her two sisters, shaking her head.

"I don't know," responded Louise, "but I sure would. Wow! It's going to be so exciting. And a new dress. Do you s'pose it'll be from the city?"

"I have no idea," spouted Angela as she dropped the last roll of dough into the big pan and smacked it hard with her floured hand.

"You are going to do it, aren't you?" asked Sara.

"Of course. For Trudie. As a friend." And then she added, to herself, *for I fear that in the days to come Trudie will need every friend she has.*

————

Angela watched Derek carefully in the days following his mishap and was finally convinced he had suffered no permanent injury. But what a scare he had given them! Gradually she ceased protesting each time Thomas suggested some heavy task for the boy. Derek didn't want to shun responsibility and looked at Angela with embarrassment when she tried to divert his tasks to herself or to one of the girls. Still, it was hard for Angela to go on as before and even harder to keep silent when she saw Derek grab his glove after a day in the field and climb onto his horse for a trip to some neighbors.

Don't slide. Don't slide, she wanted to call after him.

Seeing her anxiety, Thomas always tried to ease her concern. "The boy is fine. I've watched carefully and he's just fine."

Angela knew Thomas was as concerned for Derek as she was, and she tried to assure herself that Thomas would know whether or not there was any reason for further worry.

Eventually Derek returned to haying, manning the heavy forks, and sweating his way through the hot and dusty summer.

Angela found herself taking frequent trips to the hayfield with the excuse of bringing her brothers a cool drink or a light snack. Other years it had been Sara's job, but this year Angela wanted to keep an eye on her young brother.

On one such trip she stopped to feel the heads of Thomas's experimental grain. They were filling out, but Thomas admitted disappointment in his new seed.

"It's not quite right yet," he said. "I need to bring in another strain that has more resistance to the hot summer winds."

"You mean you have to start all over?" Angela queried.

"Oh, no. Not all over. It takes years to produce just what you are looking for—and I haven't given it much time."

Angela slid her hand over a shock of the new grain, wishing again that Thomas might be freed to work on his seed instead of being saddled to the cares of the farm. She moved on, her shoulders heavy with concern.

As she passed Charlie's shack, Charlie rose from his front porch and greeted her.

"How is he, girlie?" he asked. Angela flushed. She hadn't realized her missions had been that obvious.

"Fine," she responded. No sense denying her purpose in making trips to the hayfield.

Charlie walked along with her to the house and settled himself on the cool back porch.

"You want some cold buttermilk?" Angela offered, and Charlie was quick to accept.

Angela took the lunch dishes to the kitchen and returned with two glasses of buttermilk.

Charlie sipped slowly. His thoughts seemed to be far away.

"Been doin' a lot of thinkin' lately," he said at last. "Guess you heard thet Gus is out of a job."

Angela nodded.

"Feel sorry fer Gus. Been wonderin' iffen there's room in thet little shack fer two old duffers."

Angela pictured the two little rooms. It seemed a bit crowded to her way of thinking.

"Been thinkin' thet a fella could build on another bedroom," Charlie went on. "Right out thet there side toward the east."

Angela nodded again. It seemed workable.

"Maybe Gus would like to spend some of his money on it," Angela suggested.

"I'd forgot all about his money," mused Charlie. "Shucks— with all thet money—what'd he ever want to live with an old geezer like me fer?"

"Because you're his friend," replied Angela.

Charlie nodded then, turning the empty glass in his hands.

"I've been doin' some more thinkin' too," he went on.

He was silent so Angela prompted. "About?"

"About yer ma and pa. Their religion. What they used to say. You know what?"

"What?" asked Angela.

"I even been tryin' to live like they did." He straightened his shoulders and looked directly into her eyes. Then he seemed to sag.

"Guess I don't know enough about it—'cause I keep gettin' all tripped up. Just when I think I got the hang of behavin' proper, I go an' do somethin' all wrong. Don't know how your folks kept all those rules straight."

"You think that their—their faith was a bunch of rules?" asked Angela softly.

"Wasn't it?"

"No. No—it wasn't rules—not as you think."

Charlie seemed confused, and Angela wasn't sure she could explain it properly.

"It doesn't start with rules," explained Angela hesitantly. "It starts with the heart."

Angela remembered kneeling at her mother's knee as a child of seven. She, too, had thought she could be good by keeping the rules, but her mother had explained that it wasn't her self-righteousness that would prepare her for heaven; it was her trust in the Savior who had paid the penalty for all her wrongdoing.

"It starts with the heart," Angela said again, placing her hand over her own heart. "We are all sinners. We can't be— be good enough to earn our way into heaven—none of us. God knew that. That's why He sent His Son Jesus to pay the penalty for sin. He said that the wages for sin was death. That part He didn't change. But instead of making each one of us die for our own misdeeds, He allowed Jesus to die for us—for all of us. But even though the—the penalty has been paid, it's of no effect unless we accept it. It's like getting a—a present that you don't accept. Like you—and the will. It said that you could have the land—but you wouldn't take it. You can do the same thing with God's pardon. You have to accept it like a freely offered gift—with thankfulness."

Charlie was silent while he pondered the words.

"That's all?" he asked at last.

"Well, not quite. I mean, when we admit we're sinners, then we ask for His forgiveness and accept His gift—like I said. Then He does the rest. He cleanses us. The Bible says He gives us a new heart—a clean heart—so that we can keep His rules."

Angela groped for an explanation that Charlie might understand. Through the window she spotted a pot on her kitchen stove.

"See that pot," she said, pointing her finger. "If I pushed it over the heat and it boiled over—what would spill out on my stove?"

Charlie hesitated, chewing on a corner of his mustache.

"What's in it?" he asked slowly.

"That's it," replied Angela excitedly. "Whatever is in it spills out. That's the way it is with us. That's why we can't be consistently good if our heart is evil. As soon as things get a— a little too hot for us to stand—the evil spills out. We need to be cleansed. King David prayed, 'Create in me a clean heart, O God.' We all need that first. Then what you call 'the rules' sort of come in."

Charlie waited for her to explain.

"Even after we've been cleansed we need His help," went on Angela. "We can't do it on our own—none of us. We ask for His help—daily. Why, I remember my pa praying every morning that God would give him wisdom and power and patience for the day."

"He did that?"

"And so did Mama. In fact, I think she did it many times throughout the day. I heard a prayer on her lips so often."

Angela fell silent as her thoughts turned back to her mama's whispered prayers.

"Is thet all?" Charlie asked at last, his voice low and solemn.

"Well, the Bible says we are to be baptized—as our testimony to the Lord. And believers read the Word and pray often to get to know God better."

Silence again.

"Go to church?" asked Charlie

Angela nodded. "The Bible says not to forsake the gathering of ourselves together for praise and fellowship," she confirmed.

"I figured as how they'd get thet in there somehow," mused Charlie.

"You don't like church?"

"Know'd too many hypocrites," responded Charlie.

"You are not responsible for the hypocrites," Angela assured him. "They must answer to God for their own deeds. You are responsible only for you."

Charlie seemed to be chewing on the matter as he continued to gnaw at his mustache.

"An' thet's what yer folks taught ya?" he asked.

Angela nodded.

"No wonder I couldn't git it to work on my own." He laid a gnarled hand over his own heart. "I ain't been changed none in here—and boy, I sure do need me some changin' on the inside iffen I'm ever gonna do any changin' on the outside."

"We all do," admitted Angela softly.

"Ya got an extry Bible?" Charlie surprised Angela by asking.

"We all have Bibles. Mama saw to it that we each got one for our eighth birthday. As we grew up we could hardly wait till it was our turn."

Then Angela thought of her mother's Bible with its marked passages. It would be better for Charlie. Her mother had written little comments and explained certain scriptures. She went to get it and handed it to Charlie. He accepted it hesitantly.

"I'll take special care of it," he promised. "I know it's a heap special to ya."

Angela nodded. "If you have questions," she said, "speak

with Thomas. He's much better at explaining these things than I am."

"You done jest fine," Charlie told her. "Now I guess it's up to me."

Chapter Twenty-three

Trudie's Day

Trudie's wedding was set to take place right after the morning church service. The girls were going to dress for the ceremony at the Merrifields'. Angela had come to terms with taking part as Trudie's bridesmaid, but she was not pleased at the prospect of wearing a gown purchased by Carter Stratton. She would have offered to pay for it, but her common sense told her that this might squander the family's income for the entire year. Instead, she suffered the humiliation in private, making no comment even to Thomas.

The sun was shining and the breeze gentle as Trudie and Angela hurried to the parsonage following the last amen. Trudie, so excited she was giddy, told Angela breathlessly that she still had not seen her wedding dress.

What if it doesn't fit? Angela asked herself. In that event, there was little time to do any alterations.

"Carter made me send all my measurements in a sealed envelope to the seamstress," Trudie babbled. "Oh, I'm so nervous, I can scarcely think."

So what did he do about me? Angela wondered. She had been asked for no measurements.

When the girls arrived at the house, Mrs. Sommers had Trudie's dress spread out on the parson's bed. It was truly a magnificent creation. Angela had never seen anything so beautiful. The satin shimmered in the sunlight that spilled through the bedroom window.

195

"Oh!" cried Trudie, "look at it! It is—it is beautiful—just like Carter said."

If Trudie had not already been so excited, she may have wept. As it was she giggled like a child, and Mrs. Sommers had to prompt her to hurry and change into the wedding gown. Angela was full of misgivings about what the dress she was to wear would be like, but when she saw it, she was stunned. It was absolutely perfect.

The soft blue satin had folds and folds of skirt. The bodice was fitted and the sleeves puffed and then fitted from the elbow down. A row of delicate pearl buttons in the back went from hip to neckline. Angela wondered distractedly how she would ever get them all fastened in time for the ceremony. She asked someone to go get Louise to help. In the bedroom she slipped out of her summer voile and into the soft depths of the satin.

The dress fit to perfection, accenting her slim waistline, her creamy skin, and her deep blue eyes. She could not believe her reflection in the mirror.

"It—it's beautiful," she whispered, and for one awful moment she felt that she would never forgive Carter Stratton. Then Louise burst through the door, panting from her run across the churchyard. Her eyes opened wide and she gasped at the sight of Angela.

"You look like a blue angel!" she cried.

"Don't talk silly," Angela said curtly. "I need you to button me. There are more buttons back there than I can count."

Louise set right to work on the buttons. Even so, Trudie was already waiting, fully gowned and coifed, by the time Louise had Angela buttoned up.

"Oh, Angela. You look beautiful!" Trudie cried. "The dress fits as if it was made for you—oh, how silly of me—of course it was!"

"Thank you," returned Angela. "What a beautiful gown. And your red hair looks stunning."

Trudie flushed. "Then I guess my wedding will be the most charming event in the county," she responded. "Both of us look magnificent."

They made their way the short distance across the grassy

lawn to the little church. Angela could hear the organ playing.

Nervousness brought a flush to Angela's cheeks. She had never been in a wedding party before. She stepped to the back of the church and waited for the cue from Mrs. Merrifield; then she began the slow procession toward the altar. On her arm were white camellias and blue forget-me-nots. A spray of baby's breath was tucked in her loosely coiled hair.

As she neared the front of the church her eyes met those of Carter Stratton. He nodded ever so slightly and gave her one of his measured smiles. Angela dropped her gaze. She wasn't sure of the message in his eyes and she did not want to understand it.

All heads turned when Trudie appeared at the rear of the church. Eyes glowing, she came down the aisle on her father's arm, her full-skirted gown swishing against the sides of the pews. Her head bobbed under the satin and lace of her veil.

Oh, God, breathed Angela silently. *May she always be this happy.*

Trudie reached the front amid murmurs of awe, and Pastor Merrifield stepped forward to begin the ceremony.

Angela stood as if in a trance. She watched and listened in a daze, but soon someone nudged her and she realized that Trudie was now Mrs. Stratton. An arm was extended to her and she took it. She hadn't paid any attention to the man standing next to Carter Stratton and to her surprise she saw that he was a total stranger.

"I'm Carter's cousin on his mother's side," the young man whispered to her as they walked back down the aisle together. "And you are Miss Peterson?"

Angela nodded her head.

"Carter said that I'd be pleased to escort you," he continued, "but that was an understatement."

Angela tilted her head and studied him, wondering if he had the same controlled charm as his cousin. But instead Angela saw warm, humorous eyes, held in check by proper manners.

"And your name is?" she prompted.

"Bradley Whitteker," he responded. "You may call me Brad."

"I think I shall call you Mr. Whitteker," Angela returned, but there was teasing in her voice.

They went directly from the church to the Sommers farm. Ladies that Angela did not even know scurried about loading long tables with sumptuous-looking dishes.

The wedding couple and their attendants were ushered to the head table. There were bouquets of flowers everywhere. Angela eased her skirts gently around them. She did not want to chance any kind of soil on the expensive gown that belonged to Carter Stratton. Carter gave a short speech of welcome to the guests, then seated his bride and took his place beside her.

Angela had to admit that it was an impressive event. Everything was done in the most elaborate fashion possible. Her escort behaved himself as a true gentleman and provided her with interesting conversation, seasoned well with a dash of wit. To her surprise, she found herself enjoying the meal rather than enduring it.

At length the feast was over and the crowd started to mill about while the new couple opened their wedding gifts. Angela wanted to escape the crowd and noise for a bit and enjoy some fresh air. She moved away and took refuge under the shade of a large elm. She felt as if her hair were pinned to her scalp. She wanted to pull out the combs and just let the tresses spill about her shoulders, but she told herself that for Trudie she could endure the discomfort a few moments longer.

The day had turned warm. Too warm. Angela longed for a bit of the wind that Trudie had prayed away. The tight bodice fitted her like a corset. She would be relieved when she could slip out of the gown and replace it with her own comfortable voile.

She was tempted to sit down on the cool grass, but she could not risk getting stains on the beautiful satin. She didn't even dare lean against the trunk of the elm tree. She stood erect, wishing the minutes by so she might be released from her satiny blue prison.

"There you are," said someone at her elbow. She turned to see Thane studying her.

"Tired?" he asked, concern in his voice.

She nodded her head. "Tired and warm," she admitted, "and so anxious to—to get out of all this—these layers."

"You look beautiful," he whispered, and his eyes told her he meant the words.

Angela felt flustered. Thane had never given her such an intimate compliment before.

"Why, thank you," she managed, and let her eyelids fall to hide the confusion she felt. "The dress is—is most fashionable."

"It's not the dress," he continued. "Though you do make it look awfully good."

Her eyelashes fluttered up again. Was this really Thane speaking?

"I noticed you are wearing the cameo," he commented softly.

Angela nodded. "I like it," she admitted, lifting the cameo so she could see it too.

He opened his mouth to respond, but before he could get the words out someone called for Angela.

"I must go," she apologized, begging him with her eyes to understand.

He nodded, but as she stepped away he reached out and took her hand, halting her.

"Angela," he said, in a voice little more than a whisper. "May I come calling?"

For a moment she did not understand his question. He always came calling. Had always been welcome. Why would he ask—? And then his meaning reached through to her. Thane was asking permission to call—on her. Her heart fluttered within her chest and her breath caught in her throat.

"May I?" he asked again.

She forced herself to look into his eyes. They were pleading. Angela had never seen such a look in his eyes before.

"Please," he said again, and the pressure on her hand increased.

"I would be honored," she managed to whisper and lingered just long enough to read the relief on his face before she withdrew her hand and slipped away.

Angela didn't stop to analyze her happiness as she hummed her way through her morning chores. She just knew she felt like singing. Even Louise's bad temper at the breakfast table did nothing to daunt her good spirits. Angela coaxed the girl into better humor and sent her off to school with at least the scowl removed from her face.

After the kitchen was in order, Angela went to her room and spread the blue gown out on the bed. She carefully surveyed each inch of material. She did not want to return it in soiled condition.

She wasn't sure what Carter Stratton would do with the dress. Trudie could never wear it. She was much more "full-figured," her mother called it, than Angela.

When Angela was convinced that the dress was in mint condition, she wrapped it carefully in tissue paper and bundled it into a large box. Tucking the box under her arm, she started across the field to the Strattons'. She wasn't sure who would greet her. Gus was no longer there. He and Charlie were busy making plans for adding a room to the small cabin.

In answer to her knock the door was opened by a stiff-looking woman in a starched apron. Angela wondered if the woman and the garment had been dipped in the starch together.

"I have a box for Mr. Stratton," Angela explained with a smile.

"Mr. Stratton is presently on his honeymoon and isn't expected home for some time."

The woman even spoke stiffly.

"Yes," admitted Angela. "I know. There's no hurry about the box. It can await his return. I would be appreciative if you'd see that he gets it—after he gets home."

The woman nodded in a short, clipped manner, accepted the box and moved as though to close the door. Apparently the interview was over. Angela smiled her thanks and stepped back. She just had time for a quick glance at the new hallway. Carter had certainly changed things. The walls were papered in a leafy green pattern and trimmed with cream woodwork. The floor was covered with thick sea green pile rugs. Rich tapestries hung at the tall windows, and brilliantly colored pictures almost covered one wall.

"I think I liked it better before," Angela muttered to herself as she made her way down the brick steps.

She remembered Carter's words on his wedding day. "You must come and see Trudie often. She regards you as a dear friend."

Angela thought of the many years she had puzzled over whether she was a friend or foe of Trudie Sommers, but she pushed the thought aside. Perhaps she could be a friend to Trudie in the future, but she did hope that the visits would take place at her own farmhouse, not at the mansion-like house behind her.

As Angela started back across the fields her song returned. She was happy to be going home. Happy that her family was well. Happy that both Charlie and Gus were going to share her yard. But especially happy that Thane was to call.

Chapter Twenty-four

Commitment

Thane had sent word with Thomas that he would come calling on Friday night if it was convenient for Angela. She would not have dreamed of turning him down. After all her years of close friendship with Thane, Angela felt strangely nervous and excited.

"Stop it," she scolded herself, lifting a trembling hand to brush her hair back into a neat knot. But she could not control her feelings. She had never been this agitated when Carter was calling.

Carter! With his name came the painful memory of his curling lips and final cutting warning: "You are all set to be an old maid. No man will marry a woman who brings along three younger siblings."

The words brought Angela's hands to a halt. She clutched at the combs she was about to place in her hair.

Carter was right. No man—not even Thane—should be expected to take on a ready-made family.

Angela leaned against the bureau and shut her eyes tightly, but the tears squeezed out from under the lids.

"It wouldn't be fair. It wouldn't be fair," her heart cried. "Oh, God, if only Mama—" But Angela checked her thoughts. For the first time in her life she had been about to blame her mama for not staying with them.

Forgive me was her next cry. *I didn't mean it. I didn't. I know Mama did not will to die. I know she—she wanted to be here for her family. I know that—that she—she trusts me to take her place.*

And with those thoughts, Angela straightened her shoulders, brushed the tears from her eyes, and finished pinning her hair.

She took one more look in the mirror to be sure no traces of tears lingered, then smoothed the skirt of her blue gingham. She preferred her voile, but Thane had always been partial to the gingham.

Thane and I have always been dear friends, she told herself. *There is no reason for that to change. We can remain friends— I will tell him so.*

When Thane arrived, Sara hurled herself at him, assuming he was there just to see her. He pulled her braids and tweaked her nose and then handed her a small package of sweets. Louise stood by, grinning and blushing, and Thane paid her a nice compliment, gave Derek a playful punch on the shoulder, and turned his attention to Angela.

He did not say actual words, but Angela felt she had been paid a high compliment as well. It was in his eyes as he noted her appearance and smiled his greeting.

To Angela's consternation, Thomas moved to set up the checkerboard. But Derek, not Thane, took the seat opposite him. Angela breathed a sigh of relief and indicated that the parlor was available. Thane did not need a second invitation.

"I'll see you later—if you haven't been sent off to bed," he promised Sara, as her lip began to protrude.

"None of that," he said, pretending to tweak her nose again.

Sara grinned impishly.

"See that she gets her homework done," he told Louise in mock seriousness.

Louise nodded and then began to grin.

It was a warm evening so Angela had not asked Thomas to lay a fire in the hearth. She waved a hand to indicate that Thane could be seated on the brocade settee and she moved toward the rocking chair.

"Sit here," said Thane, patting the seat beside him. "I have something to show you."

Angela obeyed, curious.

Thane reached into a jacket pocket and drew forth a small packet.

"Pa got in a new shipment, and I thought of you," he explained. He lifted a tissue-wrapped object from the brown paper and held it out to Angela.

She took the gift and carefully folded back the tissue. Inside were two of the most delicate, dainty lace hankies she had ever seen.

"Oh, Thane!" she exclaimed. "They are beautiful."

"You're welcome," he said, and they both laughed.

"I was going to get around to a thank you," Angela chuckled. "Really I was."

Her nervousness left her. She settled easily onto the seat beside him and they talked as they had done over the years. As the evening wore on, Angela forgot all about her little we-can-be-friends speech. It seemed so right for the two of them to be there—to be sharing thoughts and dreams. She almost forgot to offer refreshments. When she went to get the tea and tarts she was surprised to discover that the rest of the family had retired.

"Why don't I just join you in the kitchen?" Thane asked. "Then you won't have to bring everything in here."

Because it was Thane, Angela did not argue. Instead, she chuckled and nodded her head for him to follow. They pulled chairs up to the kitchen table and shared the food and continued to talk.

When Angela told how frightened she had been when Derek winded himself playing baseball, Thane reached out and took her hand. It never occurred to her to withdraw it. Thane listened attentively, nodding his head in understanding, increasing his pressure on her fingers.

"He seems fine now," he said comfortingly.

"Yes, thank God," breathed Angela, and without thinking she reached over with her other hand to clasp Thane's fingers.

Thane's hold on the slim hand tightened. Then he glanced

at the clock. "Oh—oh!" he exclaimed. "I'd better get out of here before your big brother throws me out."

Angela followed his gaze to the clock and was shocked that it was almost one. She laughed and tried to pull her hands away. Thane reluctantly released them.

"I'll get your hat," she told him and walked the few steps to the wall pegs where the hat hung.

"So you are throwing me out," he teased, but he accepted the hat and then stood up.

"Angela," he said, taking her by the shoulders and turning her slightly so the glowing lamp filled her face with light, "I have enjoyed the evening—tremendously."

"So have I," she whispered honestly.

He drew her gently toward him and brushed a kiss on her forehead.

"May I come again?" he asked softly.

She could not speak. She pulled back so he could see her; then she nodded her agreement.

"Thank you." He lifted a hand to brush her cheek gently and then he turned and was gone.

Angela floated up the stairs and down the hall to her bedroom. She had never felt so—so light—so treasured—so filled with joy.

"Oh, God," she breathed as she placed her hand on the doorknob, leaning lightly against the door, "I think Mama would be happy for me."

But you didn't explain that you are just to remain friends, said an accusing inner voice that shattered Angela's peace.

"Next time," she promised herself. "We'll talk about it next time."

But the weeks passed and the visits continued and Angela could never quite remember at the right time that she had something important to discuss with Thane.

———

"I miss Thane," pouted Sara, and Angela's eyes opened wide in surprise.

"Why, he is here two or three times a week," she responded.

"But I don't get to see him. Just when he first comes. Then you hurry him off and—and hog him all to yourself," Sara continued, her lip trembling and her eyes accusing.

"Why I—I," sputtered Angela, and then admitted meekly, "I guess I do."

"Well, I think we should all get to see him. He belongs to all of us," Sara declared.

Louise nodded, for once in total agreement with her younger sister.

"All right," said Angela. "We'll have him over and we'll all share him. What would you like to do?"

"For supper," clapped Sara, her eyes now sparkling.

"For supper," agreed Angela.

"When?"

"Is he coming tonight?" asked Sara.

"Yes—but it's too late to get word to him about supper."

"But we can ask him tonight. Let's ask him for Friday. We'll have our supper and wash the dishes and play our memory game and then we'll all make popcorn and play games together."

Sara seemed to have it all worked out.

Angela nodded. "All right," she said. "You may extend the invitation."

As soon as Thane stepped through the door, Sara hurled herself at him, her plan pouring out in an excited torrent of words.

Thane looked over the young girl's head and received a slight nod from Angela. "It sounds like a wonderful plan," he said, giving Sara a brotherly squeeze. "I accept."

Sara squealed her glee, reached for the ribbons that Thane held out to her, and promised to do her homework.

"How's harvest coming?" Thane asked Thomas.

"All done for another year," Thomas responded.

"New seed produce?"

"Yeah, but it needs some more work yet. Have to add another strain. But I did get a nice bunch of seed to work with."

Thane looked over at Derek. "Hear you're still tearing up bases," he teased, and Derek glanced up and grinned. It was now acknowledged that he was the best baseball player at his school.

"How do you spell sedimentary?" asked Louise from her spot at the kitchen table.

"What are you ever going to do with a big word like that?" asked Thane, stopping beside her and looking down at her book.

She lifted her head and screwed up her face. "I have to do a report for school."

Thane spelled the word for her and then followed Angela to the parlor.

On Friday Thane spent the evening with the whole family, and even Sara seemed satisfied with the outcome.

"See," she told Angela, "it works just fine. Why don't we do that all the time?"

"Because—well—because Thane and I like to talk."

"I like to talk too," protested Sara.

"That you do," Angela agreed, but she could find no words to explain the situation to the young girl.

Louise cut in with a toss of her head. "They're sweethearts. They don't want company."

Angela opened her mouth to protest and then closed it again. What could she say? She still hadn't had her talk with Thane—and each call was bringing them closer together.

Sara had a birthday. To please her and the rest of the family, Angela again invited Thane for supper. She did not promise her family the entire evening, however. Thane had hinted that he wanted some time alone with her.

The celebration went well. Louise had baked the birthday cake and Thane praised it liberally while Louise flushed in pleasure and embarrassment.

Thane presented Sara with her first pair of soft kid gloves. Sara and Louise both had to try them on—just to see how they felt.

Thane helped with the dishes, but Angela sensed that he was in a hurry to get the task over and escape the kitchen.

"How about a walk?" he asked Angela when they finished their work.

Angela agreed. She loved to walk. It was late fall now and the evenings were cool, so she went to get a heavy shawl.

When they stepped out onto the back porch a full moon was shining. Angela stood for a moment and looked up into the heavens to get her thoughts under control.

Somewhere up there her mama was dwelling. She had been reunited with Papa. Angela felt sure they were happy. Still, she often wondered if they could see their family struggling to make their way without the example and counsel of wise parents.

Thane took her arm, and Angela allowed herself to be led around the house and toward the long country lane.

"Look at all the stars!" she exclaimed.

Thane released her arm and let his hand reach down to enfold hers. She wrapped her fingers around his large sturdy ones and walked closely enough that her shoulder brushed against him.

"Sara's growing up," Thane observed.

Angela nodded. "She's growing fast. I sometimes fear that she'll soon catch me," she laughed.

"Well, you're nineteen—almost ancient," teased Thane. "She has a long way to go yet."

Angela laughed.

They walked in silence for a few moments; then Thane picked up the conversation.

"My mama always said that a girl is old enough to know her own mind at nineteen." His voice still held a teasing note.

"You have a very wise mama," responded Angela in the same tone.

Thane stopped and turned to the lane fence. He lifted an arm to lean on the top rail, drawing Angela close beside him, still holding her hand.

"Then if you know your mind," he began, his voice serious now, "do you—are you ready to promise to be my wife?"

Angela was aware that his hands tightened on hers, but then her world began to spin. She caught her breath and found herself straining in the semidarkness to study his face. He was not teasing now.

"Do you mean—?" she began but could not finish. She should have known this would happen. She should have been prepared. She should have explained to Thane that she could not leave the children until her task was completed. She could not.

"I—I can't!" she cried, a sob catching in her throat. She saw in the moonlight the surprised and hurt look that crossed Thane's face. But he did not release her hand. He drew her even closer.

"What do you mean, you can't?"

"I just can't. I promised Mama that I'd—that I'd care for the family—"

"You can still care for the family," he interrupted. "That won't change."

"But I—I have to live with them—" began Angela.

"We'll both live with them."

"But—but you won't want to—to take on a whole family when you wed," she sobbed and leaned against him to cry.

Thane took her by the shoulders and looked into her eyes. "Angela, when I asked you to marry me, I already knew that you'd never leave them. I have always known that it would mean caring for the family. I love you, Angela. I love Thomas and Derek and Louise and—and Sara. I feel they are my family, too. But it is you that I want to marry. You that I want to share my life. You that I love."

Angela was silent while his words found their way to her mind and to her heart.

"I—I didn't know that you—cared—like that," she managed at last.

"I have always cared—like that," he assured her, gazing deeply into her eyes.

I should have known. I should have seen it, thought Angela. *It has always been there, boldly declaring itself in his caring, his eyes, his touch.* As soon as Angela accepted that fact, she knew with a certainly that Thane meant every word. She looked up into his earnest eyes.

"You gave me the scare of my life when—when you were seeing Carter," Thane went on solemnly. He drew her back into his arms. She could hear the beating of his heart as she lay her ear against his chest.

"It would have been all wrong," she whispered.

"I know," he answered. "All wrong. I'm so thankful to God that you realized it before it was too late. I have never—never prayed so hard in all my life."

Angela closed her eyes tightly and breathed a prayer of her own.

"I'm still waiting for my answer," he prompted, whispering into her hair.

"Oh, Thane," she responded, looking up at him. "I—I don't think it's a bit fair to you. It won't be an easy task. You have no idea just how hard—"

Thane's arms tightened around her. "Angela, just answer me."

"Yes—yes, I'd be happy to be your wife."

Thane kissed her then while a million twinkling stars clapped their hands above them. The moon dipped thoughtfully behind a cloud, allowing them a few moments of total privacy. When the silver glow of moonlight restored light to the world around them, Thane spoke. "Would you like to go in? We have a lot of plans to make."

Angela agreed. Her heart was singing. Her blood was racing. Her world was spinning in a flood of glorious light and color.

She lifted her face to the open sky. "Oh, God," she breathed. "I'm so happy. Tell Mama, will you, Father? I want so much to share this moment with her."

Chapter Twenty-five

One More Memory

In a way, Sara got her wish. She shared Thane. In fact, the whole family shared in the planning for their future. They held long discussions around the kitchen table. The coming marriage affected them all in more than a usual way.

"I'd like to farm," Thane said candidly. "I always have wanted to. I've talked to Pa about it. He'll help to get me started on my own place."

"No need for that," put in Thomas. "The farm is here. You may as well farm it."

"And you?" asked Thane.

Thomas grinned slowly. "I'd still like to get a chance at seed experimentation."

"Do you know where you could go?" asked Angela.

"I've written a few letters," Thomas admitted. "One university is quite interested in my projects."

Angela was surprised to hear that Thomas had already approached a school about his work.

"Then I'd be happy to farm your land—until such time as Derek might want to take it over," agreed Thane.

"I don't want to farm," Derek said quickly.

"So what do you want to do? Play baseball?" teased Thomas, reaching out to ruffle Derek's hair.

Derek blushed, then grinned. "I want—I want to teach," he said. "Maybe coach some—and sure, I'd like to play baseball. But I don't want the farm."

"Then we don't have to move!" cried Sara, clapping her hands.

"That's right. We won't have to move," agreed Angela.

"We can keep right on going to the same school." Sara seemed very pleased that her life would not change drastically.

Louise tilted her head and looked at Thane. "Will you be our new pa?" she asked.

"Is Angela your mother?" he asked in return.

"No-o-o. But she's our boss."

"Then I will be your—your big brother, and I will help with the bossing a bit, too. In place of Thomas."

Louise shrugged. She certainly didn't need any more bosses, but she didn't seem too upset by the arrangement. Perhaps she thought it wouldn't be too bad to trade one boss for another.

"You can boss me—if you want to," conceded Sara amiably.

Thane reached out an arm and drew the young girl onto his lap. "I can't imagine you needing a boss," he told her and pulled a pigtail.

The wedding was set for the month of May. Angela marked off the days on the calendar. There was so much to do and she had such limited knowledge of how to plan a wedding. Over and over she visited the Andrews household, getting much-needed help from Thane's mother.

But her usual duties still had to be cared for. The housework was just as demanding. Sara had outgrown everything she owned, and Angela spent hours at her sewing machine.

Louise still had her emotional swings from high to low. Some days Angela felt as if she was at the end of her patience. Thomas would only shrug and say, "You're a woman; you understand her better than I do."

But Angela could not recall going through such a tough time in her own growing-up years.

Mama would have known, she told herself over and over.

She would have known when to make an issue and when to let it pass.

Then she would find herself praying, "Oh, dear God, please help Sara pass through the years of change with more ease and less turmoil."

So Angela's days were filled to overflowing with scarcely time to think. Between caring for a growing family and preparing for a coming wedding, she felt as if her world were spinning out of control. Thane often came in the evenings, and Angela sometimes darned socks or hemmed skirts while they chatted. He did not seem offended that he did not have her full and undivided attention.

"I wish there was more I could do to help," he fretted. "Perhaps we should just elope."

"Mama wouldn't have been in favor of that," responded Angela, not seeing the teasing glint in his eye. "She always felt there was something special and sacred about vows taken before the Lord and the congregation."

Thane did not joke about eloping again.

Angela had seen little of Charlie or Gus over the winter months. The small addition had been made to the cabin, and Gus had moved in his few belongings and his bed roll and now shared the three-room home. Angela wondered if he did the cooking duties, but she had never gotten around to asking.

With the receding of the winter storms and the warming of their world, Charlie and Gus came out of hibernation.

"Sure good to be out in the open," Charlie said to Angela one day when she went out to feed the hens. "Man can get cabin fever all shut up like that."

"You could have come over," Angela informed him. "We would have been glad to have you."

Charlie chuckled. "Well, girlie. Seems to me thet you had about all yer evenings taken."

Angela flushed slightly but accepted the teasing with a smile.

"There were mornings—and afternoons," she teased back.

Gus approached slowly. Angela noticed that he was limping.

"Lumbago," explained Charlie to her unasked question.

"I'm sorry," sympathized Angela.

"Oh, it'll get better with some sunshine. Always does," said Gus cheerfully. "Always does."

"So why don't you come in for some coffee?" asked Angela, ashamed of herself for neglecting her two old friends.

They accepted immediately. As they waited for the coffee to boil, Charlie began to question Angela about her plans for the spring garden. Angela admitted that she had not begun to think of gardening.

"Why don't ya just give us the seed and let us go at it?" asked Charlie.

"Oh, that would be unfair—" began Angela.

"What's unfair? We plan to eat from it. We'll plant lots fer everyone. An' we still can swing a hoe. The time outta the cabin an' in the sun will do us good."

Gus nodded in agreement, and Angela finally agreed, telling them what a relief it would be to let them take over.

"Been readin' yer ma's Bible." Charlie announced a complete change of topic.

Angela raised her eyes to look at the old man.

"Understand a lot of things I didn't understand before," he went on.

Angela moved her gaze to Gus to catch his reaction.

"Gus an' me figure as how it's about time we got ourselves straightened out and attendin' church."

"As soon as it warms up we figure we'll have the preacher baptize us in the crick," put in Gus. "Right in the crick."

"Oh—but first," began Angela, "first you must make your—your commitment—to the faith."

"Did thet," said Charlie simply.

Gus nodded. "Yep. Yep. Did thet."

"You did?" said Angela, her eyes opening wider.

"Did thet," said Gus. "Both did thet."

"But how did you know—I mean, what did you—"

"Jest followed the Book," said Charlie. "Yer mama had all

the places marked—jest like ya said. We jest followed the Book."

"Jest followed the Book," parroted Gus.

"It works," continued Charlie, tears trickling down his weathered cheeks. "I got thet there new heart—right in here." He placed a calloused hand over his shirt front. "Feel changed. New. Just like the Book says."

"Yup," put in Gus, tears forming in the corners of his own eyes. "Changed—jest like the Book says," and he reached up a twisted hand to cover his own heart.

Angela had tears of her own now. To think that years after the seed had been sown by her parents, it had now born fruit. "I—I just—don't know what to—to say," she stammered. "I'm so—so happy. Papa and Mama would both be so—so pleased."

"Yup," said Gus nodding his head. "Yup."

When May arrived, Thane had joined Thomas in the fields to get all the planting done before the wedding. Feeding hungry men and sending children off to school kept Angela's already busy days even fuller. Derek took on a man's share of farm chores. Daily Angela breathed a sigh of thanks that she didn't have the responsibility of the big garden. Charlie and Gus had kept their promise, and plants were peeking their heads above the ground, already promising an abundant yield.

Thane and Angela had little time to themselves, but they promised to make up for it in the years ahead.

The morning of the wedding Angela turned to her bedroom window and was disappointed by the sight of drizzling rain. "I had so hoped for a sunny day," she mourned, and then remembered her mama telling how her own wedding day had been greeted with a shower as well.

"But by wedding time," her mama had said, "the clouds had rolled on and the sun was shining."

Angela prayed that it might be so for her and Thane as well. "But if it isn't," she determined, "this will still be the happiest day of my life." Angela rose from her bed with a song and hurried down to prepare the family breakfast.

"Aren't you the cheery one this morning," greeted Thomas as he lifted the milk pail from its hook in preparation for his trip to the barn.

Angela beamed at him.

"Have you noticed the weather?" asked Derek as he struggled into a light jacket.

"I noticed," said Angela. "To be honest, it's not what I would have ordered—had the choice been mine—but we'll make do."

Thomas nodded. "I think it will clear by midmorning," he predicted cheerily.

They hurried through the morning chores and breakfast to get an early start on their trip to town. The girls were to change for the wedding at the Andrews' house after the morning service. Mrs. Andrews had helped Angela sew her wedding gown. It was not nearly as elaborate as the gown Trudie had worn, but Angela was content. It suited her.

Louise was to wear a dress of pale blue and Sara one of soft pink. Angela was allowing Sara the privilege of pinning up her long blond hair.

"It is rushing things a bit," she explained, "so tomorrow it is back to braids again."

Sara nodded, but her eyes danced with the excitement of being considered grown-up—even for a day.

"We must hurry," coaxed Angela as they finished their breakfast. "We don't want to keep everyone waiting. Thomas, are you ready with the Scriptures?"

Thomas lifted the family Bible and was about to begin the morning reading when Louise interrupted.

"Couldn't we play the game? Just once more? Please. It won't take us long. Please."

"But we can still play the game. Just as often as we like," said Angela. "Thane is always happy to play it with us."

"But Thomas will be gone," said Louise, fighting hard to

keep back the tears. "It just won't be the same anymore."

No. It would not be the same. Thomas would be gone—
leaving for his dream of schooling and research just as soon
as she and Thane returned from their short wedding trip. And
then Derek would be leaving them to make his way in the
world. And before they all turned around, Louise would be
grown—then little Sara.

Before Angela could start crying, a new thought came to
her. She would always have Thane. There would be no day
when he would grow up and leave her. That was the marvel
of God's great plan. Through good times and bad, through
sickness and health, in weakness and in strength, Thane
would be with her as long as God granted them years on earth.
It was a comforting thought to Angela. She rose from her chair
and lifted her head, her eyes shining in appreciation for the
wisdom and love of her Father.

"All right," she agreed. "One more time with Thomas."

Louise, satisfied, settled back in her chair. Angela hurried
to the buffet drawer and came back with the fifth scribbler
they had been filling with their memories.

Thomas started the memories. "I remember," he said, "the
morning I was baptized. It was a very special morning for
me—I was telling all my friends that I intended to put aside
selfish plans and try to live my life in the manner Christ
taught His disciples. Mama took me in her arms and told me
she was proud of me for making the right decision—then she
looked me in the eyes and said, 'Thomas—always be true to
the step you are taking. Don't ever—ever think of turning
back.'"

As Angela hurriedly wrote to keep up with Thomas's
words, she noted to herself that *somewhere along the way we*
have changed from just sharing memories to also thinking of
the lessons Mama so subtly taught with each little incident of
our childhood.

After a moment of silence Derek cleared his throat and
said, "I remember one morning when I went out to feed the
chickens and the mother cat was running across the yard with
a little dead bird. I chased her and got it back. I cried—and I

brought it in to Mama. She just hugged me for a long time and let me cry and then she said, 'Son, don't fight death. Death, too, is a part of life. One thing dies that another might live. God is a wise God. He has a purpose for all things—even death. And for us—His special creation—death is the only gate to eternal life. When the time comes for me to join Him, though we might wish to linger a bit, it will be a triumphant time. Remember that.' "

Derek stopped and swallowed hard. "I had forgotten that," he went on, "until just now."

Angela blinked away tears. To some it might have seemed morbid to be talking of death on her wedding morning, but it wasn't morbid to Angela. She felt that Derek had just made an important step in dealing with his grief.

"I remember," said Sara, "the little pink quilt Mama made for my dolly. I got the dolly for Christmas and she didn't have any blankets and it was cold. I remember. We shivered even in the kitchen that winter."

Angela remembered that cold spell of which Sara spoke. It hadn't lasted long but it had been bitter.

"Well, I wanted my dolly to be warm. I tried to hide her under my sweater, but then Mama said she would make her a quilt—and she did. And when she gave it to me she said, 'Sara, always show as much—much passion—' "

"Compassion," corrected Angela softly.

" 'Com-passion,' " Sara continued, " 'toward others as you are showing for your dolly now. Share your warmth, Sara. Share your love.' "

Louise wriggled on her chair as if she had changed her mind about wanting to play the game. By the time Angela had finished writing Sara's memory, however, Louise was ready to begin.

"I remember," she said in a whispery voice, "one morning when Mama came to call me for school. I didn't want to get up so I thought I would just pretend I was sick."

Louise stopped and fidgeted some more.

"Well, Mama laid a hand on my forehead and she said there was no fever—then she had me open wide my mouth and she looked at my throat. She said it was fine. She pressed on my tummy here and there and asked if it hurt and I said 'No.' Then she asked me if I had—had broken my leg and I said 'No' again, so she said I must really be quite fine then. Nothing seemed to be wrong—so she told me to get up. After breakfast when I was kissing Mama goodbye, she held me close and said, 'Louise, don't ever try to pretend you are something that you are not. Folks always see right through the sham. Be true to others—and to yourself.' "

Louise paused for a moment and then admitted softly, "Sometimes it is still hard for me not to pretend—a little. But I—I am trying to learn."

You poor darling, thought Angela as her pen stopped writing for a minute while she considered the words. *Perhaps you are growing up.*

Angela was the only one left. She looked around the table at her family members and cleared her throat.

"I remember," she began with trembling voice, "when I was about ten years old. Mama was sick in bed and I was sent to the field to take lunch to Papa. On the way home I found some early roses. They were the first ones I had seen that spring—just beginning to open—bright and pink and sweet-smelling. I knew how much Mama loved the spring roses so I stopped to pick some. Just a little handful. That's all there were. I remember how I got some thorns in my fingers. I even got a drop of blood on my pinafore where I wiped my hand.

"Then I started on home, thinking how happy Mama would be when I arrived with the flowers. I had to cross the creek and it was higher than usual. Papa had thrown a log across it, but I wasn't very good at walking the log. I was about halfway across when I started to lose my balance. I grabbed frantically for an overhanging limb and managed to keep myself from falling in. But in clutching at the tree branch—I dropped the roses. I stood there crying as I watched the stream carry them off. When I got home I was still crying.

"I went into Mama's bedroom and threw myself against her bed and told her what had just happened.

"She put her arms around me and pulled me close. 'Angela,' she told me, 'you are my flowers. My roses. You and your brothers and sisters. You make up my bouquet. And a more lovely bouquet never graced the home of any woman. I will always—always—see you as such—my beautiful, beautiful roses. I don't need any others.' "

Angela stopped to wipe her eyes. They would be red and swollen for her wedding if she wasn't careful. At least Thane would understand.

She lifted her head and looked around the table. "And that is how I see you, too," she told them softly. "As Mama's roses. She would be so—so proud of you—if she could see you now. Just as Thomas and I are."

They leaned forward for an impromptu family embrace and then wiped away tears, smiled at each one, and rose from the table.

"I don't want to keep Thane waiting," spoke Angela softly as she replaced the Memory Book in the bureau drawer. She turned to her brother. "I'm afraid you'll need to push the team a bit, Thomas."

"Thane will wait," Thomas said with confidence, "but we'll see that you're there on time."

He stopped long enough to pull her into his arms and give her a brotherly embrace.

"You're going to make him a beautiful bride—and a wonderful wife—Mama's rose," he said softly. Then he released her slowly, turned, and was gone to fetch the team.

Be the first *to know*

Want to be the first to know
what's new from
your favorite authors?

Want to know all about
exciting new writers?
